The Birdwatcher

Also by Ethel Edison Gordon

Where Does the Summer Go?
So Far From Home
Freer's Cove
The Chaperone

The Birdwatcher

Ethel Edison Gordon

David McKay Company, Inc.
New York

The Birdwatcher
COPYRIGHT © 1974 BY Ethel Edison Gordon

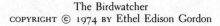

LIBRARY OF CONGRESS CATALOG CARD NUMBER: 74-77147
MANUFACTURED IN THE UNITED STATES OF AMERICA
ISBN 0-679-50446-x

The Birdwatcher

1

I've always wondered about the element of chance. I might have been born in an underprivileged country, to less comfortable parents, with some fault of birth that would have determined my life, through no fault of anybody, through no known design. But before Dan's death I had never felt what a terrifying factor chance is. It is like the presence of evil—unreasonable, fortuitous, mindless, irrevocable. The unlooked-for meeting, the suddenly twisted ankle, the delay fumbling for a house key—and the pattern of existence is altered, for better, for worse.

Like the way Dan died. The peace had been signed, Dan had remained behind his unit only to finish off some work. *If* he had gone with them, *if* he had flown in another plane, *if* a mechanic had been more careful, he might never have crashed and died. Why?

The day I learned about his death I had spent my lunch hour looking into Bloomingdale's windows. The war was over and he was coming home, and I was planning to buy a bedspread for his bed.

I was living in his apartment. I'd moved in just before he was sent to Vietnam, when we knew we would be married as soon as he came home. It was Dan's idea that I keep his apartment. It was comfortable, I could walk to work, and if I stuck my head out the window I could see the Queensboro Bridge. But most important, if I stayed there I could feel near him. I could read his books, touch his civilian suits still hanging in his closet, listen to his records, and drink his wine when I became unbearably lonesome. I could imagine I was already his wife.

Reason had told us not to marry until he came home. Sometimes now I was sorry, and so, I think, was he, from his letters. It had become important to have some tangible sign that we intended to spend our life together. Even to buy a bedspread in Bloomingdale's helped. He expected to be home within sixty days; it wasn't too soon to start fixing up the apartment. I remember how, that lunch hour, I studied one bedspread for a long time. It was quilted, with red poppies. I can remember that bedspread clearly, even though the events that followed tend to run together in my mind.

I was late and had to hurry back to the office. Beale demanded punctuality just as he demanded precision, and I wouldn't have dreamed of crossing the great Beale. Everybody knows Geoffrey Beale, the expert in the antimissile. Working for Beale is like working for Wernher von Braun. The job had opened up right after I was graduated from Smith. I'd heard about it from my Uncle Willy, who is Pentagon brass. One of the essential aspects of the job was security clearance, and Uncle Willy, who was a Major-General, vouched for me. Physics had never been my best subject, though I'd taken some courses in it, but even if I'd known more I still doubt I'd have been able to understand Beale's work. I took a battery of tests and came out rated intelligent, trustworthy, accurate, conscientious. The final test was the interview with Beale, and he chose me.

My office was in midtown Manhattan, an air-conditioned skyscraper. The salary was fine, and working with Beale would require my constant attention, which I needed to get my mind off Dan. Beale had picked me out of five well-qualified candidates, which was flattering, but after I started working for him I had no time to preen. I worked harder than I believed possible, put up with long hours and Beale's impatience and apoplectic anger, sustained by the realization that if he weren't satisfied with me he would have sent me packing mercilessly.

That day I rushed into the lobby, flashed my badge at the security policeman stationed at our elevator, and rode up to our floor of offices. My own cubicle was next to Beale's office. I'd locked the last piece of copy I'd typed in my desk before lunch. I wanted to check it over with fresh eyes before I turned it in. I sat down, put away my handbag, unlocked the drawer, and took out the copy.

I must emphasize that most of what I transcribed might as well have been written in Greek. Now and then a word seemed familiar, but it was always in the context of an incomprehensible paragraph. I knew we were part of the "smart bombs" program, and that Beale was working on the accuracy of landing on target, that was all. Beale's pages to be transcribed were usually typed crudely by him, and to these pages he would add additional material handwritten on slips of blue paper. I never knew why but I assumed his scribbled notes were afterthoughts or amplifications, and not of any special significance, and when I returned my copy to him, I did as I was instructed, clipping the blue slips of handwritten notes to the larger pages of his typed notes, all of this clipped to my copy.

So I now had to unclip the blue slip in order to reread my own pages, and it was at that moment that Judy, who is my best friend, came over to my desk with the telegram.

"This came for you while you were out, and I signed for it. Maybe Dan's on his way home. Mind if I wait and see?"

All the time I was poring over Bloomingdale's windows the wire that said Dan's plane had crashed and he was dead was lying on Judy's desk. Dan must have put me down as the one to be notified; his parents were dead, and I suppose I was closer than his brother or his aunts and uncles.

I remember staring at the telegram and feeling nothing but disbelief. Hadn't I practically picked out the bedspread for our bed? It was impossible. Why should I have been so incredulous? I must have confronted the possibility of his death. Only, the war was over now; I did not have to worry anymore. I am twenty-four years old, and nothing tragic has ever happened to me. Whenever I read in the papers about objects plummeting down and killing the unsuspecting people below, about people who miss one plane and take another that crashes, about the people who set sail on a sunny day and run into a squall and are drowned, I shudder, I feel pity, but I doubt that it could happen to me. How could it? Didn't I meet Dan and fall in love with him and he with me? My life has been a succession of sunny rooms in pleasant houses, and maids who ironed my blouses. My father died when I was too young to remember, and my mother married again, but I even loved my stepfather, and saw him for years after my mother divorced him, before he moved to the West Coast. My mother is doting, if nervous and anxious, and I found life more relaxed after I moved out of her house in Scarsdale and into my own apartment. I know I am not immune to tragedy; it is only emotionally that it seems incredible.

I remember Judy taking the telegram out of my hands and reading it. I thought of Dan who had specialized in urban planning, who was a builder and not a destroyer of cities, a man who visualized clean and beautiful places for people to be happy in. He shouldn't have ever been a soldier; he believed in peace, and the only reason he'd chosen the Air Force was that he loved flying. In his job he'd never flown a bomber. Maybe he tried to make himself believe there was some purpose to his being there: I want to think that. I remember taking the typed transcript to Beale's door, tapping, and when he opened it, saying, "I haven't read this through carefully, but I think it's okay. I'm going home now."

I remember the look on his face, and his talking in a low voice to Judy while I got my bag. I heard him say, "Stay with her until her mother comes. She does have a mother in Westchester, doesn't she?" and I remember turning to Judy, and saying, "I'll be all right. I'd rather be alone. Thanks."

I walked to my apartment, our apartment, but I couldn't make myself go in. I took Dan's car from the garage and drove uptown blindly, heading, I suppose, for Scarsdale and my mother's house, but when I came there I couldn't go in and face her sympathy. I drove on to Connecticut, and when I reached Salisbury, and the Copper Kettle Inn, where Dan and I spent what we thought of as our honeymoon, I stopped, thinking I might stay a while and remember things. But when the manager showed me to our old room and asked after Dan, I knew I couldn't stay there either. I drank some coffee and drove back to the city. The bridges? The tolls? I must have paid them just as I must have parked the car in the garage and taken the elevator upstairs. I was tired enough by this time to sleep.

My mother woke me at noon the next day.

Beale had called her, as did Judy, and she'd been trying to reach me and finally had decided I was staying with some friend. When I still didn't answer my phone in the morning, she drove down from Scarsdale.

She put her arms around me, which was bad for my determined effort to keep under control.

"Come home with me, Lisette. This place isn't good for you now."

I've always disliked my name—Lisette. I don't feel like a Lisette, which seems to belong to a bisque-faced French doll with absurd eyelashes, but my mother conceived me in Paris on her honeymoon. I've done what I could to counteract the image of a Lisette, but I'm not a large girl, unfortunately, and when Dan was being especially loving he would say I had an Audrey Hepburn smile. I've never tried to counteract that—who would even if there was a remote chance that it was true—and I must say that when Beale calls me Lisette, he gives it a no-nonsense sound that makes it almost satisfactory. But now, in my mother's tender tones, it put my back up.

"Mother, I live here. This is our home." This *was* our home.

"You could come and visit with me for a few days. Just a few days. Until you're more yourself."

Who is myself now? I will have to learn all over again.

"I'm going to send Dr. Keyser to see you. He'll give you some pills."

"I don't need any pills. I won't let him in."

Pause. Mother walked around, folded a newspaper, straightened a cushion.

"Mr. Beale has been wonderful. So concerned. Amazing, with all the important things on his mind."

Beale would have to go through the nuisance of breaking in another secretary, which would irritate him unbearably. It wouldn't be easy to find someone as conscientious as I had been about those damned equations describing his even more pinpoint precision instruments that will explode missiles even as our own were being exploded over someone else's country. I had let myself be blinded, as Dan did. The sound that came up into my throat was like a stopper forced from a bottle; my tears followed.

"Oh, my dear Lisette, all right, all right. This is good for you, now you'll feel better—" My mother held me, smoothed my hair, patted my shoulders until I forced the stopper back into the bottle.

"Would you mind—I'd like to be alone."

"I can't leave you like this."

"I'm all right now."

"I'll do some shopping and come back later. Is there anything you need?"

"Not a thing."

"But you are being stubborn, Lisette. It would be better if you came and stayed in your own home. Actually, it would be best if you left New York entirely. Would you like to take a little trip? I'm sure Mr. Beale would give you the time off. You might take advantage of Irene's invitation. She just sent another letter, urging me to get you to come—"

"I'm not up to visiting."

"She's your cousin. She understands."

"I'm better working it out by myself."

I could hear her rummaging around, putting things away in the bedroom, in the kitchen, and I closed my eyes and let her do it. I knew it was an expression of her concern. I hadn't let her do anything else; I was being bitchy, an unfeeling child, I knew. Finally she let herself out, thinking I had fallen asleep. The telephone rang often for the next few days, and after a while I began to answer it and thank everybody for their sympathy. When my mother came again, it was easier.

A few days later Edna telephoned. Edna was Beale's personal secretary. She said Beale wanted to see me that afternoon; was two o'clock all right? I never said no to Beale. I made my bed and ran the vacuum and got dressed; I even made a pot of coffee, because Beale drank coffee all day.

He rang the downstairs bell at two, and I buzzed back,

and moments later he came in, puffing and panting as if he'd walked those four flights instead of being whisked up in the elevator. He looked uncomfortable, and astonished at himself for being there at all. His face, large and flabby, with small eyes buried in folds of flesh, was coldly intelligent. He took the coffee and stared at me as he drank.

"I'd like you back at work, Lisette. Think of it not as a job but as a duty."

I don't know when the decision had been made: I wasn't aware of having made it. I heard my voice say the words without a tremor.

"I'm not coming back, Mr. Beale."

I suppose I could have saved him a trip if I'd known this was what he'd come to say. His expression didn't change.

"Natural reaction. Take a week to think it over. Take a trip somewhere and get some sun. Perk up your appetite. You're being emotional about this. Use your head."

"I know you can't get along without a secretary. Don't waste your time waiting for me, Mr. Beale. Fill the job."

His eyes were suddenly laser-sharp. "Why?"

"I don't want to work with . . . war. I don't want anything more to do with death."

"I see." And then, "Our work might actually deter an enemy. Prevent killings."

"I know all that. It's the way I feel."

"Use your head, Lisette," he said again. "What are you going to do? Type for a manufacturer of ladies' undergarments? Answer phones? Think of the job you are giving up."

"I am. I can't, Mr. Beale."

"I'm going to give you another week," he said. "You're a level-headed girl. You'll come to your senses."

He didn't leave right away. There was something on his mind that he couldn't bring himself to broach. Maybe he thought I would change my position by the sheer force of his presence. He moved around; he said, "Does your uncle know of your decision?"

"I haven't spoken to him."

But my mother undoubtedly had. My mother keeps in unrelenting touch with the few surviving members of our family. She keeps guest rooms perfectly in order down to the last scented drawer lining on the remote chance that someone in the family will be in the vicinity of Scarsdale. One day soon (I was surprised it had not already happened) my Uncle Willy would be down to see me.

Still he made no move to go. He inched uneasily in his chair, and then, suddenly, his eyes pinioned me.

"That day you left. When you brought me your typed transcript. You didn't return my handwritten notes."

I stared. "They were clipped to the copy, as usual."

"They were not clipped to the copy. I know they usually are, but they were not that day."

I said, faltering, "They could have slipped off. My desk—"

"We went through your desk. Your office. And mine. They're gone."

I didn't know what I could say.

His eyes shifted uncomfortably. "Would you get your handbag, please, and look in it?"

"But security—"

"The guard says he passed you through that day without looking. Someone had told him about your fiancé. He was being considerate, he says. You'd worked for three years, there had never been anything irregular. Sentiment is inexcusable in this case."

I brought out my handbag, stunned. I turned it upside down in front of him, and everything clattered to the table. Even the telegram. I had wondered what had become of the telegram.

"This *is* the bag you carried?"

I pointed to the telegram mutely.

He said some explosive words under his breath. He said, "Do you have any idea how important those notes were?" He swore again. "I was sure you had them, that you had simply forgotten and taken them with you. I should have come before. I was so sure you had them but had overlooked them."

For Beale this was almost incoherence. I could only repeat stupidly, "You're sure you looked everywhere?"

"Of course we looked everywhere!" he snapped. "We turned the office into a shambles! What did you think?"

"The shredding machine?"

"I initialed nothing for the shredding machine that day!"

"But you have my transcript, and I'm sure it's accurate—"

"I don't give a damn about your transcript, accurate or not! The whole point is secrecy, can't you understand? No one must get his hands on those notes!" He shook his head. "This is a disaster. A disaster."

When I let him out, he was still shaking his head, still muttering, "A disaster."

He barely said good-bye to me, let alone remembered to say even the most conventional words of sympathy. No one seemed to give Dan, or my feelings, a thought. Maybe what happened was larger and more consequential, but not to me, not then. They weren't even allowing me to give myself up to wholehearted grief, intruding on me with those damned notes so that my grief was mixed with a sense of guilt and dismay over what amounted to tragic carelessness.

The next day I had an even more upsetting visit.

Someone rang my bell and said he was from Larris Foundry. Larris Foundry was the company working on Beale's project, so I let the man in at once. I knew most of the staff, even the security people, but this one was a stranger.

He looked at me disapprovingly. "You should have asked to see my identification. *Anyone* could find his way into your apartment."

"But you said you were with Larris—"

"*Anyone* could have said that."

He produced a card and a badge. The badge showed a statue of blind Justice and read Federal Bureau of Investigation. The card said the bearer was Martin Holder, and gave a number for him.

He said, "I suggest you open your door on the chain until you've checked credentials. You're a very trusting young woman and you shouldn't be, not when you work in an office that deals with highly classified information."

His face was meaty, his eyes like flint. He looked exactly the way FBI men look on television, except that he was bigger and heavier.

He said, "You're Lisette Knowles?"

I nodded.

"You work for Larris Foundry Company?"

I said yes.

He said, "I'm here about some classified information that your company reported missing."

"I explained to Mr. Beale that I don't know anything more about it than what I told him."

"Will you please tell me everything you can remember about the day the information disappeared?" he said, bringing out a notebook.

I talked while he listened and wrote, his face showing no expression. When I finished, he said, "You went to an inn called the Copper Kettle. In Salisbury, Connecticut. Why?"

I stared at him. I had forgotten to mention that. How had he found it out?

He was waiting for my answer.

I tried to explain my state of mind, but it was hard to tell if he believed me.

But he went on. "I'd like the names and addresses of everyone who visited you since that day you left work."

That was easy. Just my mother and Judy. And, of course, Mr. Beale.

"Have you searched your apartment carefully?"

"I've looked everywhere it could possibly be."

He said, "Would you allow me to check?"

When I stared at him in disbelief, he said, "You understand, I didn't come with a search warrant. In order to get one we'd have to go to a magistrate with our evidence, and we don't have any concrete evidence. But it would make our job easier if you'd let us proceed without the warrant. All you have to do is sign this, which is your permission to let us search. *If* you're willing to cooperate."

"Of course, I want to cooperate," I said numbly. "Do whatever you have to do," I said, signing. "Shall I leave?"

"You can stay," he said, pocketing the paper.

It took him two hours, and it was an experience to see him work. He tipped out coffee grounds and opened the toilet tank; he stood on a chair to feel behind cornices and into the lighting fixtures; he even turned the garbage out onto a newspaper and then replaced it neatly. There wasn't a single item in a single drawer that he didn't shake, press, prod. I don't know at what point the belated realization came to me, but when it did my cheeks grew hot with outrage.

"Do you think I *hid* the notes? Deliberately hid them?"

"Routine, Miss," he said, not even turning his head.

"Then you must think I'm a thief. Or a . . . a traitor."

Even saying the words out loud sounded melodramatic and absurd, but was it more absurd than watching this man handle my most intimate possessions?

"It's my job, Miss Knowles," he said stolidly. He finished and came back into the living room and wrote some more in his notebook. "Sent anything to the laundry or the cleaner? Sent any letters or packages by mail?"

"If I were a spy, would I tell you?"

"No need to get sore, Miss. I'm asking the routine questions."

"I haven't been out of the apartment."

14

"Give me the name and address of your laundry and dry cleaner anyway, for the record."

I managed to remember them.

"If you haven't been out, do you have food brought in?"

"Enough was here, from before. I haven't been exactly ravenous. And my mother brought me a few things."

He wrote it all down.

I said tightly, "Does anyone really think I took those notes? Does Beale?"

He said, as if I were a slow child, "You might have done it without thinking. You were in a state of shock, maybe."

"I was not."

"We think you were," he said, still stolidly. "You'd be surprised what people do when they're in shock, and they don't remember a thing afterward."

"I would know if I'd taken them. Or if they had turned up since."

He went on as if he hadn't heard me. "Miss Knowles, why don't you intend to come back to work at Larris Foundry?"

I shut my mouth tight. "That's my business."

He consulted his notes. "You told Mr. Beale that you don't want to do any work connected with the national defense. Does that mean you feel hostile toward your country?"

I didn't know whether to laugh or to cry. "Look," I said, trying to retain my self-control, "the man I was going to marry was killed last week. No one seems the least bit interested in that, or in me, or in how I feel. But in view of that fact, would you think it unreasonable if I don't want to have anything more to do with death or destruction? Maybe I didn't realize the implications of the job when I took it, maybe I tried to believe I was helping Dan, but I can't go on with it now anymore. But that doesn't mean I want to hurt my country!"

He went on stolidly, as if he hadn't heard me. "The information on those notes could be immensely valuable to our enemies. We believe they'll try to get hold of them."

"But how would they even know the notes were missing?"

Again he looked at me as if I were feeble-minded. "*You* know. Beale knows. His secretary Edna Wilson knows. Your friend Judy Persons knows. Which means that people whom you know will know, and the circle widens. It's my job to warn you, Miss Knowles, that the enemy will be likely to contact you. And that means you're in danger, whether you have the notes or not."

I listened to him, but it was as if his words were too bizarre for me to grasp. Already I was beginning to feel that the walls of a trap were closing in around me, the bait, cowering inside. Almost without thinking I blurted out, "I won't stay here. I'm going away."

He didn't seem to catch the high note of desperation in my voice. He stood up to leave. He said, "Before you go anywhere, make sure you let us know how we can reach you if we have to. I don't think you'll need clearance at this stage, but we will want to know exactly where you are at all times."

He put on his hat at the door and said, "Thank you and

good-bye." Even he might have spoken some words of sympathy, but sympathy was not in his mind. I was used to it by now and no longer felt aggrieved. I watched him get into the elevator, but though he saw me, he looked resolutely past me as if I were a case he had dealt with and filed for future developments.

I knew now that I must get away, far away from this unbelievable situation, where people could see me for what I was, Lisette Knowles, almost twenty-four, average citizen newly bereaved and with a need to mourn without being distracted by national security and suspicion and guilt, a medium-sized young woman with what had once been called an Audrey Hepburn smile by a man who loved me and was undoubtedly prejudiced, who could never by a stretch of anyone's imagination be suspected of being a spy.

I still didn't think of going to my cousin Irene's.

2

*T*he next day it was my Uncle Willy's turn to appear at my door. He was in civvies, but he couldn't look other than the complete military man. He kissed me, he squeezed my hand in sympathy and said it was a damned shame about Dan. He accepted a Scotch and water, and told me he was on his way to my mother's house.

"It isn't like you to be so damned careless, Lisette," he said fretfully. "Still, under the circumstances it's understandable. I suppose."

"I'm positive I clipped that blue strip of paper to the copy. I couldn't have done anything else."

"I'm afraid I feel involved, you know. I did vouch for you."

"I haven't disgraced you, Uncle Willy. Honestly." My throat tightened. "I haven't defected, or anything like that."

"Stop talking nonsense," he said even more fretfully. "The fact is, you've put Beale's entire project in an anomalous position. The whole point is secrecy. Beale was onto some new precision laser honing device, and the ABM program was vitally concerned."

I'd known it was part of the ABM, and I'd seen the words *laser honing* and *missile return*, but everything else had been gibberish to me. I told that to Uncle Willy.

"I had only the vaguest notion of what it was, myself," he said. "But I did know it was devilishly important. I'm not blaming you, Lisette. Anyone getting a blow like that, with Dan, is bound to think fuzzily, but you must see now that you've simply got to remember what you did with them."

"I don't have them, Uncle Willy."

He clamped his mouth onto his glass and finished his drink at a gulp. He said, "Pack your things and come with me to your mother's house."

"No. Thanks."

"She wants to mother you."

"I can't think of anything that would be worse for me."

"Then come with me and stay there for other reasons."

"Such as?"

"For God's sake, Lisette! You *know* why. You're in danger here."

"Who's going to protect me in Scarsdale? My mother? Bertha?"

"I wish you wouldn't argue," he said. "If you were my daughter, I'd pack your bag for you and drag you there."

"Ha ha," I said. "That I'd like to see. You dragging Irene anywhere."

He retreated, mumbling, "She's a married woman now."

"When did anyone get Irene to do what she didn't want to do?"

"Irene grew up without a mother to guide her," he said. "Beck always said you were a joy to raise."

"I'm grown up now too, Uncle Willy." And as good as married. And my as-good-as husband is dead. I swallowed, and changed the subject. "By the way, where is Irene now? Mother told me, but I forgot."

"She's in a godforsaken part of Scotland," he said. "The Shetland Islands. Some distance north of the northernmost part of the mainland. That husband she has keeps her in the most outlandish places. Three years in the Middle East. I only managed to see her once between planes. It's as if he wants to have her all to himself."

I could understand the Middle East. Eugene, Irene's husband, was president of Atico Oil, which probably had interests there. But why the Shetlands? I asked Uncle Willy.

"It's the probability of oil in the North Sea. But that doesn't mean Eugene has to be there any more than he had to live in Teheran. He seems an odd fellow, and chooses to live in an unorthodox way. I'm sure Irene expected to spend her time in more civilized places, like New York or Paris or London. I often wonder if she can be happy. You know Irene. The only things that ever interested her were fashion and the theater."

"She isn't an idiot, Uncle Willy. You make her sound that way."

"I never said she wasn't bright. She is. It's just not her

kind of life. Ponies and sheep and herring. My God. To give her credit, she doesn't complain in her letters."

I've always admired Irene, as well as been fond of her, and she had seemed destined for a spectacular life. I hadn't guessed it would be marriage to an important man like Eugene. She was audacious as well as beautiful, and had always known exactly what she wanted. She was a highly paid model when I was still at Smith, and I no longer saw much of her, and she'd already done three months of an off-Broadway play when Uncle Willy invited her to go to Paris with him on Pentagon business. She met Eugene in their hotel, where he had come to a conference. I'm sure she must have heard about Eugene Farrar, one of the youngest presidents of a major company, and a bachelor; I'm sure she contrived their meeting. Irene would do something like that. And once they met, the conclusion could have been anticipated. How would he not be attracted? She was tall, with her mother's Swedish features and complexion, bright, and amusing. If she made up her mind to marry an oil millionaire, he didn't have much of a chance.

Uncle Willy was saying gloomily, "Married eight years and still no babies. If they had babies, they might have a reason to come back to the States to live."

"I can't see Irene surrounded with babies."

I hadn't meant it as disparagement, but I saw Uncle Willy's eyes flicker, and the corners of his mouth turn down. "She hasn't been well, I gather," he said. "Eugene thinks the quiet of the Shetlands will be good for her."

"What's wrong? Mama didn't say anything."

"Irene hasn't said anything. I suppose she doesn't want

to worry Beck or me. Eugene has had her to a variety of doctors, and they can't find anything wrong with her but tension and fatigue. So Eugene writes. They led a pretty gay life in Teheran. Maybe it was too much for her, all that partying."

Irene thrived on parties. I couldn't imagine they were ever too much for her. But Uncle Willy was getting ready to go. He tried one more time.

"Look here, Lisette, I've got a car and driver downstairs. He'll wait while you throw a few things into a bag."

I shook my head. "Not now. I'll be out to see my mother later in the week."

He said thoughtfully, "Have you thought of getting away and staying with Irene for a while? Beck tells me she's invited you often, which is more than she's done for me. I rather like the idea of the two of you looking after each other."

"I'll think about it, Uncle Willy. I promise."

The idea was already planted in my mind. I still wasn't sure what would be best for me, if maybe getting another job in New York might not lead me more easily back into my old way of life. Going away was running away, and I didn't want that. I didn't entirely like leaving before the notes were found, and I was sure that they would be— it was the only plausible outcome. I didn't like leaving under a cloud. So I still read the employment notices every day, though I didn't follow any up.

My mother visited me before I managed to get to Scarsdale. I could see at once she had something to tell me, but she made herself a cup of tea before she could bring herself to disclose it.

"Lisette, I haven't wanted to worry you, but I think you should know. The FBI has been to my house."

I hadn't told her about their visit to me so as not to worry her, because she does get upset easily, but now I admitted that they'd been here, too. "It's only routine, Mother."

"Only routine?" she cried. "It was humiliating! Naturally I gave them permission to search when they asked me, how could I not? They'd think I was a spy! I had to make Bertha swear she wouldn't tell a soul! I felt like a common criminal! Worse! A *subversive!* He searched the house from top to bottom! I was only afraid someone might drop in while he was there. How would I explain it? Lisette, he warned me that enemy agents might break into the house! Lisette, you must get away!"

"Mother, if they were really after me, they'd find me, wherever I went."

"I've called Uncle Willy. I think we should have police protection."

"Oh, *Mother.*"

"Uncle Willy said it wasn't feasible. I think I will go away myself, stay with Aunt Frances in San Diego. But I can't go unless you go too, Lisette."

I took a deep breath. I was being pushed into going, and it was harder than ever to say no now.

"I'll think about it, Mother. Maybe I'll go down to a travel agent and get some ideas."

"It's dangerous for you to be alone. If you went to Irene, you'd have the protection of their household. They probably have a great many servants, and you know how difficult it is to get into a rich man's establishment."

"I don't fit in with Irene's grand life, Mother. I'm not in the mood for it now anyway."

"Irene understands. She'll be very sweet, I know."

"I suppose you told her all about Dan," I said.

"Of course!" she cried. "How would Irene feel if I didn't?"

My mother and Irene kept up a voluminous correspondence. Irene has always been like a second child to her. Irene's mother abandoned Uncle Willy and their daughter when Irene was only ten, and for a while Irene was moody and cried constantly. My mother kept her with us whenever Uncle Willy had to be away, so that I think Irene felt our house was her home too. I must say for her that she's always been grateful to my mother. A shower of gifts keeps arriving for her from wherever Irene is, and sometimes my mother shakes her head ruefully at her house, which is losing its eighteenth-century mahogany integrity under a barrage of hammered brass and copper pitchers and jewel-studded hangings.

"Families can be a great source of comfort."

"I don't want her inviting me because she's sorry for me."

"Be fair, Lisette. She's been inviting you ever since she went to Scotland."

"She didn't invite me when she was in Teheran, going to all those parties with movie stars and millionaires."

I was being unfair again, because Irene knew I wouldn't leave Dan, or even my job. I sometimes said things to stir up mother, like a small child, I knew, but my mother's world was so firm and unshakable, and everyone's place so fixed in it, that sometimes I enjoyed jarring her convictions.

She said, hurt, "Irene has always been more like your sister than your cousin. I can tell from her letters how deeply she feels for Dan, and how much she'd like to do anything to help."

Staying with Irene was probably the most sensible plan. I would never feel completely safe, traveling alone or staying alone. Still, I didn't commit myself, not yet. Not until Irene telephoned.

I had been out. I had gone to Rockefeller Center about a job, and walked home slowly, considering what to do if they decided to give it to me. I could hear the telephone ringing while I was still outside, and rushed in, wondering if they could have made up their mind that fast.

"Lisette Knowles?"

"Yes."

"I have an overseas call from Lerwick, Scotland. Hold on, please." A Scottish voice mingled with the American operator's, and then I heard Irene's voice.

"Lisette?"

"Irene! I can't believe it's you! I—"

"Lisette, I have only a minute. This call has taken ages to get through and I expect Eugene back any moment. Lisette, I'm so sorry about Dan."

"I know. Thanks."

"I can't talk properly now. I don't want Eugene to know I've called you, pleaded with you. I don't want him to think it's so terribly important to me. He'll wonder. Lisette, you have to come. I know how sad this time is for you, and it's not fair of me to put my own problems in front of that, but you would save my life if you came. Literally."

I listened in disbelief. It didn't sound like Irene, always assured and unshaken, always in control. "What's wrong, Irene?"

"I'm not well. I'm not at all well."

"You must have a doctor—"

"It isn't like that. I can't begin to explain. Lisette, do you care for me at all? If you do, you'll come. Oh, there's the car. He'll be looking for me. I've called from the hotel here so he can't trace the call. Lisette, say you'll come. Right away. Please, I'm begging you to."

"Of course, if it's that urgent—"

But she had hung up.

I replaced the receiver, my head whirling. I must say that for the next few hours her call drove everything else from my mind. What did it mean? What had happened? Why shouldn't Eugene know she had phoned me? I couldn't talk it over with my mother. She would call Irene at once or else call Uncle Willy, and evidently Irene did not wish anyone to know of her desperate situation. Except me. How could I not go?

But I delayed. There were so many details to be taken care of. Passport. Subletting the apartment. Tickets. I did not want to fly. At that moment I thought I could never set foot in an airplane again. I would have to take a ship. Which ship? The man in Rockefeller Center called and said they'd like to try me out. I had to tell him that I couldn't accept the job, something had come up. The man seemed disappointed, and told me to give them a ring later on, in case there was a change in my plans. So

I knew I would go. It was simply a matter of getting myself to move.

But then things started to move on their own.

There was another telephone call from Scotland. A man's voice, dry and impersonal, introducing himself. Eugene Farrar. I was so taken aback I could only faintly answer.

"Irene tells me she has invited you to Scotland. I may be able to facilitate your coming."

"That would be great," I heard myself say.

"Have you filled out a passport application, taken a photograph? As soon as you've submitted it, I'll have my office in New York go to work on it. Would a flight in about a week or two be all right?"

"I prefer to go by ship."

Pause. "Ship? Doesn't matter which. My office will take care of that, too. You can expect them to send you a ticket as soon as your passport has been approved."

"Thanks very much. I don't know what to say."

Pause. "Irene thinks it might be good for you. We're all very very sorry about what happened."

"Thanks," I said again.

"Wire us when you leave. Irene's here. She wants to say hello."

I waited with trepidation. But her voice was the old Irene's, without a tremor.

"Lisette, darling, I'm so glad you decided to come. It isn't gay here, but it's different, and you may find it interesting. Eugene is going to take care of everything. He can do it so much faster than you can. See you soon, darling. I can hardly wait. I'll write you at once about what to pack."

Her letter came in the next few days, and sounded like the Irene I knew. It made a joke about the need for warm sweaters and rubber boots and my own hair curlers; I could almost see her face as she wrote. Eugene had added a postscript.

"You'll be getting your passport by the end of the week. The *Queen Elizabeth 2* sails for Southampton Friday morning and arrives on Wednesday. Since you don't want to fly, I have booked you onto the steamer from Aberdeen to Lerwick. The steamer sails twice a week, Tuesday and Thursday, so if you take the train in London immediately on your arrival you will be able to make the Thursday crossing instead of having to spend five days in Aberdeen."

The tone of his note was as impersonal as his voice on the telephone had been, as if some coldness had seeped through his angular handwriting. I wondered. It was almost as if he didn't want me to come. But maybe remoteness was the normal manner of the president of an oil company. I didn't know, I'd never met one before.

I almost missed the postscript on the back of the page. "There will be another guest with us, Jim Baird. He is trying to arrange to sail on the *Elizabeth* with you, and if he succeeds at this late date, he will look you up."

I think my first reaction was irritation. I hadn't bargained for company on the trip, and was rather looking forward to a complete break with anything or anyone that might remind me of home. True, I didn't know him, or he me, but with company I might not feel the separation as strongly as I wanted. Besides, if I didn't like him I would be trapped with him for five days in the confining, inescapable quarters of a ship. Irene and Eugene had no right imposing someone on me without first asking me.

And then I had second thoughts. I supposed they had believed it would be good for me not to travel alone, considering my probable state of mind. I imagined Jim Baird to be someone like Eugene, perhaps rich and important and remote, and he might be just as happy to leave me on my own as I would be. Anyway, he might not find accommodations; I understood the ship was fully booked. In any case, there was nothing I could do about him.

The necessary thing was to be with Irene. As the days went on, it seemed incredible that she had spoken to me out of such desperation. Could I have been wrong, could I have misinterpreted her words? But she had said I would save her life if I came . . .

In any case, it was important for my own peace of mind to get away from the apartment and from New York.

3

*T*he day before I was to sail I phoned Martin Holder at the number he had given me for the FBI offices in Manhattan. He wasn't in, but a man said he would call me back in an hour. He did, and I told him I would be sailing for Europe in the morning.

He said, "Can you send me a copy of your itinerary?"

"I have no itinerary. I'll be staying with my cousin in the Shetlands." I felt defensive enough to do some name-dropping, telling him whose daughter Irene was, and whose wife. If he was impressed, or even reassured, I had no way of telling. I went on with an attempt at firmness, "Are you or any of your investigators going to follow me to the Shetlands?"

"As far as we're concerned, you're clear," he said. "If we had any reason to think you weren't, you probably wouldn't be allowed out of the country. But I'd like to warn you again. You may be followed, and it won't be by our organization. If anyone does contact you about those notes, it's to your advantage to get in touch with us immediately. I can't stress enough that you may be in danger."

I confess I still thought he was exaggerating my position, I still felt its total unreality. I hung up the telephone and finished my packing. My mother had returned some outfits that she'd had cleaned and stored in her house, which she thought might come in handy in the cool climate of Scotland, and I had to fold them away. One of them I recognized as the suit I had worn my last day at the office, and for a moment I hesitated: should I include it? Even handling it made my heart heavy. But it was a wearable suit, and I might as well learn not to be neurotic about it, so I folded it carefully and closed the lid of my valise over it.

Most of the afternoon was spent in shopping for a raincoat with a removable lining to take care of all weather contingencies. I was able to find one, fortunately, and returned home carrying it with me. Our doorman, Murray, stopped me before I could enter the lobby.

"There's a guy waiting to see you, Miss Knowles. He says you don't know him, so I thought to be on the safe side I'd ask you first. In case you don't want to speak to him, you go right on through, and I can tell him you're not back yet."

I was more primed for panic than I had realized. My head turned involuntarily, and my heart began beating fast. Through the doors I could see a tall, fair man in a light jacket over a turtleneck shirt. His hair came neatly to the top of his collar. English? German? Scandinavian? If he were trying to look like an American, he was almost successful. Something about him . . . too good-looking to pass unnoticed in a crowd . . . But I was staring too long. I didn't want Murray to notice my alarm, and I said as casually as I could, "I think I'd rather not see anyone. Too much packing to do."

"Sure thing," he said, holding the door open for me.

I went through the lobby without turning my head, and reached the elevators. Almost as soon as I pressed the button, the door of one of them opened, and I hurried inside. But the tall man had risen and moved swiftly. He managed to slide in as the doors closed. We were sealed in the elevator cage together.

My thoughts jumbled frantically. Push past him and press the emergency button. Scream. Pretend I had a gun in my handbag. Blow the police whistle Dan had bought for me as a joke—

"Lisette? Lisette Knowles?"

My mouth fell open.

"I'm Jim Baird," he said. "I almost didn't recognize you. Irene's description put me off."

I let out my breath. I said faintly, "You're Jim Baird." I even managed to produce a smile. "Why did it put you off?"

"She said you'd be on the skinny side, and probably wear a ponytail. She was right about the smile, though." He studied me thoughtfully. "She said it would be wide and happy."

I've filled out somewhat since Irene saw me last, and I haven't worn a ponytail since high school. "I'll get even with her when I see her," I said. The elevator had stopped at my floor, and the doors were opening. "Would you like to come in?"

"I thought you'd never ask."

His eyes watched me unabashedly—bold? curious? just innocent?—as I fumbled for my key. He was more than merely good-looking; he seemed to have a restless vitality that shone through his eyes, that was in his speech, in all his movements. I covered my own interest with a hurried question.

"Do you live in New York?"

"Actually, I don't live anywhere. I've just flown in from the Coast, where I've been visiting my parents. Friends have promised me a bed for the night, but they're still at work."

I opened the door, and he followed me in.

I stopped.

How can I explain my apprehension? There was nothing tangible I could point to, and yet I sensed the room was not as I had left it, that someone had been in it recently. A man's smell, cigars maybe, or shaving soap, or a well-used woolen suit—I think I probably stood still like an animal, sniffing an alien presence. It was Jim Baird looking at me oddly that roused me.

"Sit down, won't you. Will you have a drink? There's some Scotch. And wine."

"Scotch is great."

Even as I went across the room my eyes took in the breakfront drawers not quite closed. I've been brought up to close drawers neatly. And there was the valise on my bed, with the latches closed this time. I had deliberately left them open because I hadn't been able to find the key and was afraid I'd not get it open again. "Give me a second to hang this away," I called while I went through the valise hurriedly. My quilted jewelry bag was partly unzipped, but the few pieces of jewelry I own, some gold bangles, the pearls my mother gave me when I graduated from Smith, the present from Dan of a pendant with sapphires were all there. Whoever had searched my valise wasn't interested in a few hundred dollars' worth of jewelry.

When I went to the kitchen for the glasses and ice, even here I could see someone had been through the cupboard that I had cleaned out and arranged this morning. The FBI had searched, and cleared me, they said, and I saw no reason to disbelieve them, so it had to be someone else, then, who was searching for those notes. But I must act as if nothing had happened; I brought the tray into the living room and fixed us both a drink, and tried to resume a normal conversation.

"Have you ever been to the Shetlands?" I asked him.

He shook his head. "I wonder why I'm going. Irene said it was very bleak. She warned me that if I expected a summer of fun and games I wouldn't find it at Skeld House."

"Skeld House?"

"It's the place they've rented. A sort of manor house, she wrote me, built by one of those plunderers of the past who always seem to descend on remote places and get the land and the wealth away from the natives. The man who owns it now is a present-day plunderer, owns a number of fish-freezing plants, and welcomed the chance to let the Farrars have his house so he could get off and find a bit of sun and warmth."

"You've made up your mind not to like it."

"Not quite. A lot depends on the company." He looked at me and lifted his glass. "Things are definitely looking up for the summer."

"Thanks." Maybe it was only gallantry, but he made me feel as if he meant it. There was a pause, and again I plunged in to fill it. "How well do you know Irene?"

"Not too well. I met her after she came to Teheran with Eugene. Actually I'm a sort of distant cousin of Eugene's. My father was his father's cousin. I've been with Atico since college, mainly in Teheran."

"Are you on vacation?"

"I quit about a month ago. I didn't seem to be getting anywhere. I kept after Eugene to put me somewhere more interesting, with room to grow, but he stalled until I thought maybe if I did something dramatic like quitting I could make my point. So I visited my family in California, and looked around for a job."

"Did you find anything?"

He lifted his shoulders. "My father convinced me my future was with Atico, and he may be right. He thinks Eugene is bound to come up with an offer. Atico has a debt to my father. You see, he sold them some device he patented, and they made a mint out of it, out of all proportion to what they paid him. They did offer me a job as soon as I got out of the Army, but I'm sure they didn't expect me to be satisfied with it for the rest of my life. I've made it clear to him that I deserve something better, and I have an idea he'll come up with something this summer."

"You'll have plenty of opportunity to speak to him."

36

I thought he nodded dubiously. "You've never met him?"

I shook my head.

"When his father died, he left him a third of the shares in Atico, and the board elected him president. He was only thirty, which gives you some idea of the kind of man he is. I never thought he'd find time to fall in love, and as hard as he did. But even married, he never found too much time to play."

"I wonder how Irene manages. She loves to play."

"He never stopped her, from what I hear. She led quite a gay life. I wasn't part of their circle, just one of the hired hands—" he grinned, "—but now and then I'd get invited to the boss's house for dinner or a party. Speaking of that," he said, "will you have dinner with me tonight?"

I hesitated. So far, I thought I had been successful in concealing my alarm at the realization that my apartment had been entered while I was away, but it was too much of a strain to keep up. "I have so many last-minute things to do—"

"Shall I pick you up in the morning?"

"My mother is driving down from Scarsdale to take me to the ship."

He rose. "See you on board, then. And thanks for the drink."

I leaned back against the door when he had left. It couldn't have been the FBI again; they had already searched, and said they were satisfied. It had to be some other agency, then, foreign . . . and hostile. If they had found nothing, would they not next approach me directly? How? When?

But I would be out of the country tomorrow, and maybe they would have no way of knowing where I'd be going. Even as I told myself this, I knew it was a childish hope.

When I boarded the ship in the morning, my mother went ahead through the visitors' gate and I went up the gangplank alone. I remember pausing over the strip of dark, oily water between ship and pier, filled with the uneasy prescience that this was a fateful step I was taking, that with this most ordinary of journeys I would be altering my life irrevocably. I remember faltering; I told myself I had never been psychic before, and then an officer's hand reached out to help me onto the ship—committed.

My mother was impressed with the cabin Eugene had provided, with the baskets of candy and flowers signed with his and Irene's name, furnished, no doubt, by the same efficient staff that had expedited all the rest. I would have preferred to pay my own way, but it had seemed ungracious to refuse, and I sensed it was a way for Irene to express her eagerness for me to come.

And my mother was delighted when I told her about Jim Baird, as I knew she would be. "I'm so glad you'll have company. I hated the thought of your traveling alone after the dreadful business about those notes." She added, "Could I meet him?"

His name wasn't on the First Class passenger list in the cabin so I telephoned the desk and got his cabin number in Tourist Class. We were entangled in a mesh of corridors trying to find his cabin when the announcement came over the loudspeakers: "Will all visitors kindly leave by the main deck? The ship is about to sail—"

Reluctantly, she turned back. At the head of the gangplank her face saddened, for saying good-bye, maybe for thinking the same thoughts that came to me, that it might have been so different, Dan and I might have been sailing together. I promised to write often, and she went down, insisting on waiting in the heat of the pier below for the ship to sail, which would not be for another half hour. I returned to my cabin and unpacked quickly, and then went out to the open deck to attempt to find my mother in the crowd of faces below.

The railings were jammed, and I had to wedge a place for myself. People shifted, and as soon as a few inches of space was cleared, somebody else slipped in. I was squeezed between a stout lady in a pants suit and a nun in short habit. I had promised to wave a yellow scarf, which I did, blindly, and almost at once my mother's navy-blue-and-white scarf fluttered back—our signal. I composed my mouth into a happy smile, which I hoped she would see.

Below, the ropes were being cast off, so archaically, it seemed, for such a monster ship. The sun beat down. Now and then a current of fresh sea air overcame the smells of tar and gasoline from the West Side Highway. The gangplank was wheeled away. Someone pointed, and above our heads the British flag rose to the height of the mast.

Propelled by tugs, the motors quiet, we moved imperceptibly, but the space between ship and pier was widening, and my mother's scarf was growing smaller and smaller. The blast of the ship's whistle was repeated by other harbor craft, saying good-bye. In spite of my state of mind, I was stirred, and felt my throat thicken. We reached the center of the East River, the wind whipped up, the motors began to throb. I moved with the rest of the passengers to the opposite rail, to watch the Statue of Liberty coming up.

That was when I noticed that my handbag was gone.

Again, panic. In it was everything I needed for the trip: passport, tickets, travelers' checks, my driver's license, and some cash.

I stopped; I told myself that everything could be replaced except the cash, and there wasn't that much to worry about. I told myself it was just a matter of getting duplicates for all my documents and buying a new handbag. I told myself Jim Baird was on board and could tide me over in an emergency. I hunted each foot of the deck I might have walked on, while the Statue of Liberty receded and the Verrazano Narrows Bridge skimmed the ship's smokestack, and finally, giving up, I went down to the cabin to see if it might be there. I looked everywhere, fruitlessly, and then decided to report it the purser. Hurrying along blindly, I bumped into Jim Baird.

"I was just coming to look for you. I boarded late, and just assumed you'd be in Tourist with the rest of us ordinary people."

"Irene and Eugene insisted on paying for my ticket, or I would have been," I said. "Look, I'm on my way to the Lost and Found, if there is one. My handbag is gone."

"I'll come with you. I knew when they said your name

was Lisette that you'd be the sort of girl who was always losing a glove or a handkerchief."

"But I never lose anything!" And then I thought of the notes, and I suppose my face showed the unpleasantness of that memory. I finished lamely, "It's only when I'm upset."

"And you're upset about something," he said quietly. "I could see that yesterday when we met."

We were at the Main Desk, and I did not have to answer. The officer in charge made sympathetic sounds, and promised to post a description of the bag.

"It's bound to turn up. We rarely have a theft on board."

"My passport and tickets—"

"Yes. Well, you'll have to see the purser, but give it till morning. I have a hunch it will straighten itself out."

The loudspeakers were announcing lunch. Jim said he had missed breakfast in his haste and was starved. He said he wouldn't attempt to eat with me since the tables would have been assigned, but he was sure we could be together in most other places; the *Elizabeth*, he'd heard, was not so strict about separating the classes. I went down to my cabin to wash up.

The half inch of strap showing between bed and wall was the first thing I noticed. I leaped for it, and tugged. It was my handbag; it must have slipped down partly and wedged there.

I looked through it, and everything was there, and as I had left it. For a moment I reflected: was I going to start at shadows from now on, suspect even the most innocent of events? I *might* have closed the latches on my valise last night, I *might* not have been as precise in my tidying up as I had thought. I had probably allowed the handbag to slide off the bed; after all, I didn't go to Europe every day, either. That was why when the second incident occurred I made myself put that out of my mind, too.

It was a wonderful five days. Jim and I sat together on deck, swam together, met for a predinner drink in one of the bars (I wasn't sure which one of us was not where we belonged), and we danced most of the evenings away in one lounge after another. We saw flying porpoises humped high over the waves, even a whale, and somewhere off Newfoundland we all lined up at the rails to see a tiny iceberg that seemed incapable of being a threat even to a rowboat, but which the deck steward assured us we were very lucky to avoid. The voyage was the hiatus between past and future, a suspension of time. It was good for me; it was healing.

When we neared Europe the weather turned cold, and the northern sky stayed light till eleven. The last night out the friends we'd made and Jim and I exchanged addresses, writing them solemnly on scraps of paper torn from someone's notebook and filing them away, even though all they'd be used for, most likely, would be to send each other Christmas cards next winter. The gala over, Jim walked me to my cabin and went to his, and we agreed to meet at the Customs shed under our initials in the morning.

I was too stimulated to sleep; I went up on deck alone for a last look at the North Atlantic. Someone had said earlier that we'd passed Bishop's Rock, that first glimpse of Europe off the coast of Cornwall; already the small twinkling lights of fishing boats dotted the black water. The deck was too well lit for me to see into the darkness, and I climbed to the topmost of the decks where the officers quarters were and the lifeboats. The wind was blowing a gale up here, whistling deafeningly. I found shelter between the lifeboats and strained to see the land. The wind was making a mop of my hair. I had a scarf in my evening bag, and pulled it out to cover my head. As I did so, out flew the scrap of paper with all our addresses on it and was swept away by the wind.

I looked after it ruefully, but then, to my surprise, it plastered itself flat on the wet deck. Catch it before it blows away again. As I started after it, my long evening skirt was held back, probably twisted on one of the stanchions beside me. I tripped, and fell forward on my knees. For a few moments all I was concerned with was my torn skirt and bruised knees. I could have imagined a shadow and the sound of running feet: it would have been impossible to hear anything distinctly.

A man and a woman, striding arm in arm, came up behind me and helped me to my feet.

"Deck's too slippery for walking alone," shouted the man. "You could be blown away. Lost something?"

"Just something out of my purse." The scrap of paper was no longer on the deck. It had probably blown overboard.

"Gone forever, I expect," shouted the lady. "Oh dear, you've torn your skirt."

They insisted on taking me down to the cabin.

"A needle and thread, and you can take care of the rip," said the lady. "Sure you're all right?"

I assured them and thanked them and locked my door behind them. It meant nothing. It was an annoying accident, and that was all. I reminded myself about not starting at shadows, and when I met Jim in the morning I said nothing, and didn't expect to say anything.

The ship had tied up while we slept. After breakfast, we cleared customs on board, changed money, and now we went down into the new Ocean Terminal and collected our luggage and heaved it up on the counter to be checked. It was strictly a formality, I could see: the only people opening their valises were returning British nationals. Americans were asked only if they had anything to declare. Jim finished first, and joined me.

"What is your name, please?" the customs man asked me.

For an instant I was startled: no one else had been asked his name. I told him what it was.

"Would you mind opening your valises, please?"

I felt my face redden. People were turning to stare at me, and even Jim regarded me with curiosity. I unlocked the valise and the small overnight bag, nevertheless, keeping my eyes straight forward. The man felt through my things deftly without disarranging them, and then he prodded and banged on the bottom.

"They're checking to see if there's a false compartment," Jim said. "Say, are you the American connection?"

"Oh, please shut up," I said under my breath.

He laughed, but I was near tears. I had to turn my handbag out on the counter, and I could see the people I'd sat next to on deck turning their heads to look at me as they went toward the boat train, wondering, no doubt, what kind of person they had innocently befriended.

The customs man merely said sorry and thank you as he scrawled something on the bags and nodded to the porter. We silently found our seats in the compartment and rode to London. Jim knew his way about in London and suggested the first thing we do was get our train tickets to Aberdeen, so we taxied to King's Cross and bought them for the sleeper that evening, which left us almost half a day to sight-see. We managed to see both Westminster Abbey and the Tower of London before we returned to the railroad station. We had a pleasant dinner, and he made a point, I thought, of not mentioning the incident at customs, though I was sure he must be thinking about it.

We went to our berths early, and I propped myself up on pillows to watch the unending green countryside slip by in the clear twilight, the occasional village buried in a fold of hills with only the square Saxon church tower showing, the factory town dark except for a sprinkling of cold lights, chimney pots climbing one behind the other, ending abruptly in more green countryside. I fell asleep before we reached Aberdeen, but I don't know when.

In the morning we left the station and went directly to the docks, and in the small shabby office of the North of Scotland, Orkney, and Shetland Island Shipping Company I had my ticket stamped and Jim arranged for his. There were no more berths left, but Jim said he'd nap in the lounge. It was all right, the man said, to put our baggage on board even though we weren't to sail until four, so Jim put his valise with mine in the narrow slot of a cabin I was to share with another lady, and for the rest of the day we wandered around the docks, watching the loading and unloading of a variety of small ships. We found a place for lunch, and then returned to the *St. Clere,* our ship, which was now putting aboard oranges from Jaffa, breakfast cereals from Michigan, and Danish beer, which must have represented luxury to the islanders far out in their cold sea. The wind had a bite, but the sun was warm, and I was buttoned comfortably into my raincoat.

"Going to Lerwick on her?"

An old man standing beside us spoke.

"Like the sea, do you? Most Americans take the plane."

"*She* likes the sea," Jim said. "Given the choice, I'd fly."

The furrows in the old man's face regrouped themselves into a smile. "Around Aberdeen we say: 'No time to spare, go by air, but you're sure to get there on the *St. Clere.*'"

"Is it often rough?" I asked.

He grinned again. "A wee bit of Scotch in the bar, and ye'll not notice."

Toward sailing time a crowd began to gather, men in caps, women in shapeless cardigans, the man who'd checked our tickets writing busily on a clipboard, a group of young men saying good-bye to someone leaving, shouting up to him on deck, someone playing a mouth organ. The song he played had a mournful sound to me, a long-drawn-out, weeping sound. I felt my throat tighten.

And then suddenly we were moving, and the long gray sheds began slipping past us swiftly. A woman below walked beside the ship, wiping her eyes on her sweatered sleeve. The people on the pier seemed to stare after us soberly. Departures are always a kind of death. I shivered. The gray stones of the breakwater dropped away, as did the tiny lighthouse at the tip of it. Gulls swept across the ship, mewing, a pure, unblemished white in the sunlight. The low green coast of Scotland kept pace at our left, until it was blotted out by a thickening mist. And then the wind whipped up, harshly, and the boat pitched and shuddered, steadying itself. We were out in open sea.

I had looked for this moment, I had wanted to make a complete break with the past, but I was unprepared for the sense of desolation that filled me. I felt my eyes fill, for Dan, for my own anomalous position, for the danger that seemed to lurk all about me.

Jim said, "Could you use a shoulder?"

I tried to smile.

He said, "Did anyone ever tell you that you smile like Audrey Hepburn?"

It was too much. I couldn't even answer him. The fog was thick as rain now, wetting our faces, beading our hair.

"How about a drink?" he said. "You need some cheering up."

So I followed him down yellow varnished corridors into

a small smoky bar, already crowded, and we found two seats on a bench.

"Ever try malt whiskey? Let me bring you a taste of Scotland."

I watched him gratefully as he went to the bar to order, his fair head taller than any of the others, and I wondered how I could have made this trip without him. He brought back two glasses, and touched mine with his.

"To the best of summers."

How I wished it could be! The malt whiskey was rich, like a liqueur.

"Feel better?" he said. "Maybe you'd like to talk, tell me why you're scared."

"I'm not," I protested weakly.

"You were scared of me when we met; you went into your apartment that day as if you thought it was mined, or someone was hiding behind a door ready to spring; you keep looking around as if you think you're being followed—"

I tried to laugh. "That's silly—"

"They searched your luggage at customs," he said gravely. "That isn't silly."

I finished the drink. It had warmed and relaxed me.

"Don't tell me if you don't want to, of course," he said. "But maybe it would help to talk. And maybe I could help, too."

And so I told him about the notes and the FBI's warning and how I had thought him to be an enemy agent and why I thought my apartment had been entered and searched. I didn't tell him about the two experiences on board ship: they could so easily have been just innocent, and I didn't want him to think I was only being imaginative. Irene knew about the notes, I was sure, because my mother would have told her, and if Irene knew, Eugene knew, and someone was bound to let something slip sooner or later. Besides, what difference did it make? If an enemy knew about the missing notes already, then it was no secret.

And it was curiously easing to blurt it all out to him. He listened attentively and sympathetically until I had finished, and then he said, "Let's have another drink first, shall we?" I agreed, and he brought two more small glasses and gave me mine.

"Of course, it still might be your imagination, as you say. When you're in a hurry and have things on your mind like sailing for Europe, you can't be sure if a dish is out of place or your valise is shut. Even that incident at customs—they do spot-check at times. They may have had a tip about drugs, and young people are more suspect than others today."

I nodded. I did *want* to believe it.

"The FBI is not likely to send a man out of the country after you unless they have pretty good evidence. And they did tell you they felt you were clear."

I nodded again. We sipped the drinks in silence.

He said thoughtfully, "Why do they think you have them?"

"At first they thought it was accidental, that I might have taken them home in my bag without thinking."

"That's not so unlikely, is it?"

"But they searched thoroughly, and I did, too. It's impossible." I hesitated. "And then they began to wonder. I made no bones about not wanting to work in anything to do with weapons and war. They think I'm . . . bitter about Dan's death. They think . . . I'd like to get back at my country."

He said, "Are you bitter, Lisette?"

I said sharply, "You mean, did I take the notes and do I plan to sell them?"

He reached out for my hands and covered them with his. "No, I don't mean that at all," he said. "You've been through an ordeal, but don't bristle at me. I'm a friend, remember?"

After dinner we went out and walked the narrow decks, shrouded in that luminous white batting of fog. Somewhere beyond us the sun was shining, still high in the sky, making the fog pearly, like a shell held up to the light.

He said, "You have to try and forget everything that happened. We'll all be there with you, and nobody can hurt you. I give you my personal guarantee."

When I let myself into my cabin at midnight a stout old lady was snoring delicately in the lower berth. I undressed and climbed the ladder to my ledge of a bed, marveling at the lightness of the sky even at this hour, and then, as if I wanted only to obliterate the bleakness of my mood, I fell asleep at once.

4

*M*y cabinmate woke me before six, groaning cheerfully as she laced herself into an ancient corset. "A bonny morning," she said. "Warm."

I mumbled good morning and climbed down from my shelf to look out the porthole.

We were already tied up at the pier. The gray stone houses of Lerwick seemed to rise sheer out of the water, rosy in the morning sun. The town was a cluster of slate roofs and chimney pots, the harbor dense with bobbing fishing boats and a tangle of masts. Gulls wheeled, or lined up on the rooftops like a carved frieze.

Passengers were hurrying past the porthole, leaving the ship. I dressed as fast as I could and made my way to the gangplank, a valise in each hand. Jim was below on the pier, looking up for me. He met me halfway down, taking my luggage.

"Had breakfast?"

"Not yet. I didn't know whether to take the time."

"We'll leave the bags in the shipping office and find

somewhere to eat in town. The car isn't here yet, so they probably figured we'd have our breakfast first. Someone said there's a hotel up this street."

My cabinmate had called it a warm morning. Actually it felt more like a fine October day at home. The strong salty wind that whipped through the streets brought an oddly pleasant smell of fish.

The hotel was made of the same cut granite as all the other buildings; the dining room on the second floor looked out over the rooftops. They gave us a superb breakfast of oatmeal and kippers and bannocks, and we ate everything they brought. The sudden despondency that had overcome me last night had vanished, and I was feeling a rising excitement.

When we started down the hill again, we could see a gray sedan parked beside the shipping office.

"It's Eugene," Jim said. "I thought they'd send the chauffeur." He seemed surprised.

We quickened our steps. I was curious about Eugene, about the man Irene had married. He would have to match her in some way, be spectacularly handsome as she was, or distinguished, or brilliant, have some quality other than his money and position to attract her.

I wasn't prepared for the man who met us: a quiet-looking man, not as tall as Jim, brown hair, gray eyes, dressed in a brown tweed jacket, corduroys, and sneakers. He kissed my cheek almost shyly and shook Jim's hand. He and Jim together put the luggage in the trunk.

"Shall we go?" he said. His voice, quiet and reserved, matched the rest of him.

He apologized to me for Irene not being there. "She

was still asleep, and I didn't want to wake her. She sleeps badly."

"How is she?" I would not say anything that would betray the panic I'd heard in Irene's voice over the telephone; my question was casual.

"I think the air and the quiet up here are what she needs," he said. Only that.

He drove easily, like someone who enjoyed driving. Jim filled the silence with an account of our meeting, omitting any reference to my suspicions, which was thoughtful, making a joke about my thinking he was trying to pick me up. Eugene smiled politely, but I had the feeling his mind was elsewhere; it was as if he had made up his mind to be a good host for Irene's sake, and to make the best of our presence. He asked if my cabin had been comfortable and if it had been a smooth crossing; he asked Jim how his father was. His profile was fixed firmly straight ahead, and when he turned toward me I felt it was with a cool and objective curiosity, without the warmth he might have felt for his wife's cousin. I found myself thinking of the young men Irene used to bring to our house occasionally; they were always lively, always finding some reason to laugh, like Irene. But then, maybe it was Eugene's difference that had attracted her.

The road had been skirting the harbor, past shops and sheds and drying nets, but now it swerved inland. Abruptly, the gray-stone town was gone. Here was open country, rolling fields covered with what seemed more like moss than grass, and distant hills. We passed a truncated tower of stones, set in an outer ring of crumbling stones, set in another ring half buried in the earth.

I turned my head to look as we drove past.

Eugene said, "You're looking at a *broch*. They go back to the Bronze and Iron Ages, I'm told, and were supposed to have been built by the Norse who settled here. It's pretty certain they were used as lookouts and fortifications. They're mainly found here in the Shetlands."

"I think I'd like to come back and see it better. Is it far from where we're going?"

Again that appraising glance. "You can see it when you drive to Lerwick, as you probably will. But the best one of all is on a small island called Mousa, and that would make an interesting trip for you." He said, "Actually, we have a *broch* on our property. It's in bad shape, and the Department of Monuments, or whatever they call the people who look after these things, haven't thought it worthwhile doing anything about it."

Talk ended for several miles.

Jim said, "How's the drilling?"

"There's a portable rig in Lerwick you could have seen. I'd turn around and show it to you, but Lisette is probably anxious to see Irene. The oil's here, we know that. The problem is in how much it's going to cost to extract, and can we build the equipment to do it efficiently."

The sunlight had dulled. Or was it only the look of the country? The soft green moss was gone, and the earth was scored and blackened, as if it had been burned.

"What's happened?" I gestured.

"That's peat," Eugene said. "Half the island is peat."

The top layer of grass was cut away, and the peat was cut in long meandering channels, like scars. I became aware abruptly that we were no longer seeing trees, only scattered bushes grown as boundaries, or huddled against a cottage. Clouds were lower, gray, silver, black. The sea kept appearing and reappearing, sometimes open, sometimes in narrow inlets we had to skirt, up one side of it, down the other. Sometimes we were at water level, sometimes high above it, on cliffs of white rock and scored earth.

"They're rather like fjords, these inlets, except they call them *voes*," Eugene said. "A Norse word. There's still a good deal of Norse blood here."

Peat, mossy fields, soiled tan heaps that turned out to be grazing sheep, once or twice a pony, like a toy, covered with matted brown hair. A village was no more than a cluster of half a dozen houses, a wooden pier stretching into mirrorlike water, a few brightly painted boats drawn in. When the sun cast a brilliant shaft through the clouds, when it dazzled on white headland and blue sea, it seemed to lift the spirit. When it was all gray light and desolation, I wondered how Irene could ever be happy here.

I thought of her letters from the past and the glittering existence they described, in which I was sure she was equally glittering, with her own beauty and her new wealth and position. She wrote of sandy beaches and yachts, and this movie star and that jet-set celebrity whose name even I was familiar with; she wrote of parties where the food was flown in from France and the entertainers from New York and London.

Maybe it was this place that had provoked her imploring cry. Then, why did they stay? What reason could Eugene have so compelling as to make him ignore her unhappiness? In her letters, what had she ever written of love, and marriage? I tried to remember. I couldn't. I brooded. But maybe I had underestimated Irene. Maybe it was enough for her to be here as long as he was with her.

I lost track of time. We must have been driving for more than an hour when Eugene pointed. "There's Skeld House."

The image in my mind was confounded again. A manor house in Scotland would have turrets and flying pennants and sit among beech forests. Skeld House stood alone on a rise of ground, without a tree to soften it. It was square and made of whitewashed stone, smaller than I thought, with chimneys rather than towers. A fence of stone guarded it and the outbuildings, which came into view as we rode up—stable, garage, greenhouse, sheds. A formal lawn lay in front, with neat flower beds, the flowers smaller and paler than I had noticed in England. The driveway of crushed stone crunched under the tires as we stopped in front of a weatherbeaten wood door. Windows glittered coldly. The wind sang under the projection of the eaves, the only sound to be heard.

Jim broke the stillness. He laughed. "If you were looking for the direct opposite of Teheran, you've found it."

The door had opened, and a man in a dark coat came toward us to take the luggage.

"This is Jarvie," Eugene said. "Miss Knowles. Mr. Baird."

Jarvie's lined face smiled pleasantly. Small and wiry as he was, he managed our four bags at once. We followed him into a small entry where coats hung and boots and umbrellas filled a trough, and then into a large square hall, whitewashed and cold. Several doors lined it, all closed.

Almost at once a woman appeared. I thought her to be in her fifties, neatly made, with graying hair twisted in a braid around her head.

"Mrs. Wall. Our housekeeper."

Her nod was polite and perfunctory, but her glance at both of us lingered, penetrating. "Your rooms are ready, if you'd like to go up. Jarvie is taking the luggage there."

I had no wish to go to my room. Jim shrugged.

She said, "There's a fire in the drawing room. It'll be warm, if you're chilled."

She went to one of the doors and opened it. The long room beyond had whitewashed walls and a bank of casement windows glazed with colored glass that gave the light a cheerful tint. A sofa and chairs were drawn up to a stone fireplace wide enough to have contained them. The fire burned steadily, as if it had been going for some time.

"This is for me," Jim said, and went toward it.

As I followed him, I heard Eugene say in a low voice, "Is Mrs. Farrar up yet?"

"She was dressing. Shall I bring coffee?"

"Please."

Filled suddenly with the aimlessness that comes when you've been on a long journey and now have arrived to find yourself without purpose, I wandered restlessly until I came back to the windows and opened one. Beyond were the humps and hillocks of moorland, empty and still.

"Good walking country," said Eugene, coming up beside me. "Below is Colla Voe. You'll see seals there." His voice was disinterested, polite. "If you continue in that direction you'll come to the *broch*, ours. We had this man up from Edinburgh to look it over, and he said what a pity these things were neglected. He said anyone that wanted to could take the stones for their own houses and walls, there was no one to stop them, no one who understood the value of these ruins. There isn't any wood, you see, and it's expensive when it has to be shipped—"

"Lisette!"

I turned. Irene ran toward me and caught me in her arms. For a moment we held onto each other, laughing, and saying the disjointed things people say at meeting. And yet I felt moved to tears to see her again in this strange place after so many years. When we broke apart and I could see her face, I noticed that she had cried a little, too. But it wasn't her tears that struck me. I had to drop my eyes to conceal the shock I felt at her appearance.

She was thin to the point of gauntness, so that her eyes seemed shadowed and hollow. She was still beautiful, she would always be, I think, and she had contrived to camouflage her wasted look with rouge and a bright lipstick, with a thick sweater coming to her chin, belted over heavy slacks.

She said, "I wouldn't have known you. You've become very pretty. Oh, does that sound backhanded? I didn't mean it that way! But you stayed a schoolgirl for so long!"

Her voice was the same: low, breathy, suggestive of sex.

"I don't even have a ponytail anymore," I said, smiling. She turned to Jim. "You told her. How could you?"

58

He bent and kissed her cheek. "Lovely as ever, Irene."

"Come now, how can I trust you ever again?"

She turned back to me. "Everything is going to be so much nicer, now that you're both here. It *has* been dreary. How can anyone live here?"

"People do," Eugene said.

"They've been born here, maybe they have no choice."

"And maybe some of them are even happy here."

His eyes rested on her as if she were someone he did not know very well, not as if he had known and loved her all these years. It made me uneasy, as if I were glimpsing something I had no right to see. Irrelevantly, I thought of their not having children. Out of choice? Whose? My mother had described his infatuation with Irene; could it be possible he could not bear the thought of her getting large and awkward, for even those few months? It seemed more likely she did not want anything to interfere with the high key of her life. Maybe that was why he had brought her to the Shetlands.

"Here's coffee," Irene said. "It can't be as cold as I feel. I never seem to get close enough to the fire."

Mrs. Wall put the coffee on the table near the hearth, and poured. Irene did not look up, or thank her.

Jim had been talking about floating rigs.

"We're moving in a second, about an hour's drive from here," Eugene said. "They waited for the weather to settle."

"Also the Ekflo type?"

Eugene nodded. "We're still experimenting with the deep-water stations, watching how the other companies do. There are several up north already. Question is, how well do they function in the high winds and the kind of seas they get?"

"Jim, please don't spend all your days with Eugene!"

"Not likely," Jim said. "My father was the scientist in the family. Eugene, I had a vague idea there might be some work for me here, a nice change after Teheran. I'm not so sure I'd want to stay, now that I see it. It's all right for you and Irene. You have each other."

I happened to be looking at Irene and Eugene as he spoke, and again I had the uneasy feeling that I was seeing more than I should. Eugene's face remained impassive, Irene sucked in a corner of her lip. Suddenly the atmosphere was oppressive. The silence lengthened. I did not even need the evidence of Irene's frantic phone call to know that something was wrong in their marriage.

Mrs. Wall returned to ask Irene if she would have breakfast; Irene dismissed her with an abrupt shake of her head. Mrs. Wall asked each of us in turn if there was anything she could bring, and we told her we had breakfasted and thanked her. It was Irene's manner to Mrs. Wall that troubled me. It wasn't like Irene at all. She had been raised by a housekeeper, and I remembered the easy, affectionate relationship they'd had, as if Cora had been someone in the family rather than a servant in the house. They still corresponded, my mother told me, and Irene sent Cora a regular check beyond what Uncle Willy paid her. It wasn't like Irene to be cold or arrogant, as she was with Mrs. Wall. I wondered if living in the Middle East and being wealthy had changed her.

Jim was driving with Eugene to watch the rig being installed. I was invited, almost as an afterthought.

"Thanks, no. Irene and I have years to catch up with."

"Some other time, then."

He did not kiss Irene; he said only, "We'll be back for dinner."

She did not lift her head to look after him.

We heard the sound of the tires crunching on the stone driveway, the sound of the motor receding. Again the silence. Irene drew her legs up onto the sofa and clasped her knees.

"Now," she said, looking at me somberly.

🌼 5

She did not give me time to come up with something to say. "It's all over your face," she said dryly. "You're thinking: he's horrible to her, and she's a disaster."

My cheeks must have reddened; it's not easy for me to dissemble. "I've only just met him. And you couldn't be a disaster if you tried."

"Lisette, you're a sweetie. You always were. Transparent, but lie as much as you want, you make me feel better."

Mrs. Wall returned for the coffee tray. Irene dismissed her with a disdainful gesture, waiting pointedly for the door to close behind the housekeeper before she said, "That woman is always watching me."

I was taken aback. "She does? Why?"

"She spies on me. For Eugene."

"Irene. Honestly."

She said, "And now you're thinking: Irene is losing her mind."

"Stop being silly. You're overdramatizing, Irene. Why

should I think that? All right, I don't understand why she should spy on you, for Eugene or for anybody else, but I'm sure you have some reason to think so, or you wouldn't say it."

She almost smiled. "You're so sensible, Lisette. You're what I need. Someone who'll look at things sensibly."

"Why do you think she's spying on you?"

She held out a box of cigarettes. I shook my head, and she lit one for herself. I noticed with dismay that her hand trembled. "One of the more interesting reasons might be that she's in love with Eugene."

"Irene, she's old. And plain."

"I didn't say he was in love with her, only that she was with him." She shrugged. "It isn't impossible. She was with him before we were married. He takes her with him wherever he lives. They might have slept together at one time. Fifteen years ago she must have been more attractive. I do know she resented me from the beginning."

I tried to laugh to lighten her mood. "Is this what loneliness does to people?"

She did laugh a little, too. "Maybe you'll help me to see things in a different way, Lisette." But then her laugh died away, and her voice sank. "But how can they be different than they seem? I'm not imagining them, I know that. You don't know what a relief even this is for me, Lisette. To talk. I've had no one in this whole godforsaken place to tell how frightened I am."

I said it casually. "Why are you frightened?"

She took a breath. "I must go slow. I want to make sense. It's terribly important to me that you believe me, no matter how bizarre it sounds."

64

"You know I'll believe you."

"Darling. Yes, you will. And that will help me to survive. That's what I'm trying to do now. Survive."

I promised to believe her, but I found myself listening with increasing uneasiness. I would have to be careful that she didn't sense my doubts. She watched my every expression.

I said, "When you telephoned me that first time, Irene, you sounded so frantic. Desperate."

"I am," she said quietly. She stood and went to the door and locked it, shrugging her shoulders when she returned to the sofa. "I'm frightened of everyone and everything. Those I know. And those who might be near, hiding. Waiting."

The sun came out blindingly just then, lighting the room with color from the stained glass, as if to contrast with the darkness of her words. Through the window I'd left open I could see the moors lit by long slanting rays, as in the Doré illustrations of the Creation.

"Has it only been since you came here?" I asked.

"It started before."

"Did you want to come here?"

"Why on earth should I?"

"Then why did you?"

"Because he insisted. I tried every way to persuade him. I told him I'd rent a house in London. Even Edinburgh. His private plane is at the airport, in Sunburgh. He could get anywhere in an hour. But he insisted that I come here."

I tried to understand. "Why should he make you do

what you don't want? Why did you let him make you come?"

She looked away, her mouth twisted. "For one thing, he was going to come here no matter what I did, whether I came or not. And Lisette, I do want to be with him."

If that were so, then my impression must be wrong. Why should he be insistent, why should she come? They must still need to be close to each other. Her next words showed me how foolish that hope was.

"I know Eugene. He never does anything without a purpose."

"But what purpose? Stay on here if you're not happy—"

"He wants—" She turned her face away, and I saw her eyes redden. I waited, helpless, until she got hold of herself. She said, "You have to believe me, Lisette. It's so terribly important that you don't think I'm crazy. Or lying. But—I think he wants to destroy me."

In spite of the warmth of the fire, I felt my skin prickle with cold. I tried to speak calmly. "You must be wrong."

"Look at me. Do you think I am?"

That the change in her was drastic and frightening, there was no doubt. The picture in my mind of Irene was of a girl who moved through life with an almost radiant sureness. You wanted to stay near her, as if some of that quality could rub off, be contagious, that confidence that life was a ball and beautiful, that something wonderful was just about to happen. Instead, this frightened, trembling woman was a stranger.

I said, in a low voice, "But I thought . . . he's in love with you."

66

"Over. Years ago."

"But . . . he insisted you come here. Be with him."

"I told you. He has his reasons. They don't have anything to do with love."

Her glance flicked me.

"You've stopped believing me. I know."

I had been thinking, she may be having a nervous breakdown. I'd had no experience with nervous disorders, I knew only that such people believed they were being hounded, persecuted, in danger of their lives. I knew I would have to act calmly, as if I believed her. That seemed to be important to her.

"Why should he want to destroy you?"

"Oh, he has his reasons. *I* am the reason."

She stared down at her hand on which she wore a large emerald-cut diamond, turning it so that it caught the firelight, and glinted. Irene has always loved jewels. I've never forgotten that when she was sixteen and I was eight, she had told me that she would never wear a diamond unless it was larger than her finger. I remember then marveling at her seriousness. This diamond was larger than her finger.

"I suppose I just wasn't bright enough to comprehend Eugene, the kind of man he is. He'd told me he'd never loved anyone before me. Oh, as a kid in his teens, yes. And then he was taken into the business and it was all-absorbing. When his father died, he became president. He wasn't thirty. He was considered a prodigy. He had had women all this time, I don't mean that, but he fell in love as if he were a boy. It was consuming."

The ring sparked fire as she turned it.

67

"How could I understand that? My own experience has been so different. Love was fun. Never so intense. Underneath all those business preoccupations, maybe because of them, he was a romantic. He drew up a will before we were married with an irrevocable clause. If we were man and wife at his death, I was to get everything. It was the only other way he had to express his feeling. He told me that he had forgotten such happiness was possible. It was ridiculous. I have to say it, Lisette. What woman deserves that kind of love? How could anyone live up to it?"

Her somber eyes asked me to respond. What could I say?

"I'm not perfect. I don't know how to love that way. I had lovers, before. It didn't seem like the beginning to me. I suppose I was overconfident, too. And maybe, after a while, even bored."

Color came up into her face. "There were other reasons, too. He didn't care for the social life that much; I went out alone, often. Eugene didn't mind. He said he wanted me to enjoy myself. He was busy during the day, seeing people, traveling around. Atico bought oil in the Middle East. He didn't have to be personally involved, but he was. He was always home with me at night. We were never apart, at night. If he couldn't get back, he would ask me to join him, and I did. It was the days that I had to myself. And there were always idle, attractive men."

She tightened her mouth. "Yes, you guessed it. There was someone."

"How could you?" I said, in spite of myself.

"I wasn't really in love with him. We often played

tennis together. One day I went to his house with him, we had some drinks . . . I'm not excusing myself. It was inexcusable, I suppose. Especially it was inexcusable to someone like Eugene."

"How did he know?"

"He found us together. Someone told him. It had to be Mrs. Wall. She spied on me even then. She knew whom I was seeing. She might even have paid off Lucien's servants to call her."

"But you don't know for sure."

"What does it matter if it was she or not?" she said impatiently. "It doesn't matter *now*. I wanted him to get rid of her at the time. He refused. It was the first time he had ever refused me anything. It was the way things were to be from then on. That great love of his was over. Oh, Lisette, if you knew how terribly humiliating it was! I felt exposed and shameless, a naked, yowling alley cat. For Eugene to see us . . . his image of me . . . I can't bear to think of it."

I said, "Didn't he want a divorce?"

"I wanted it. How could I live with him then? Rather, how could he live with me? It was Eugene who said no, who said we would try again. I thought he meant it, I thought he might even love me enough to forget what happened. But it wasn't that way at all. He didn't want me to get away scot-free."

I stared.

"I had humiliated him," she said in a low voice. "He was going to see that I was paid in kind. As long as I lived with him and he avoided me, I was degraded. Humiliated, as he had been. For a while it was enough. But he kept brooding. He wouldn't let me go, and yet he despised me. I think that was when he began to think the only freedom for him was if I were destroyed. Maimed. Disfigured. Even dead."

I found words. "Then he's sick. Or mad."

"Is that so impossible to imagine? Oh, maybe for you, Lisette. You've always been so sheltered. Nothing has ever happened—" She stopped, her hand to her mouth. "No, that's not true anymore. I'm sorry. Forgive me? But even so, this is different. This is . . . ugly."

"Irene, are you sure you're not imagining—"

"I have no proof, if that's what you mean. Everything could be imagination. Nothing points to Eugene. He will never be blamed for my death, when it happens—"

"Stop talking like that, Irene."

"I almost did die," she said. "The first time it was obviously an accident. So everyone thought."

She was standing now, looking down at me.

"I wrote Aunt Beck about the car."

"She told me. But you weren't hurt. Mama kept saying how lucky you were." I paused. I said, "He wasn't even with you. Weren't you going to meet him, or something?"

"It was one of those rare times when he couldn't come home. He telephoned and asked me to join him with the car, we'd drive back together in the morning. I was so happy. I was sure it was a good sign. The road was through a mountain pass. Fortunately I was going slowly, and usually I'm a fast driver. But that day I couldn't wait, and started out too early, and then I slowed down so I wouldn't arrive too soon. That saved my life. There's only the flimsiest of guard rails in the highest places, and the turns are beastly, like a corkscrew. Suddenly I couldn't turn the wheel. I was heading for the guard rail and the ravine beyond. I think I shut my eyes and tried to brake. It wouldn't have helped, I was so close, but by luck there was a jog in the road, a projecting boulder. My wheel was crushed against it, and it stopped the car."

"But it could have been an accident, Irene. It could have happened to anyone. You might have lost the power-steering fluid. It's almost impossible to turn the wheel without fluid."

"Yes, it could be just as you say. You're logical and reasonable, and I'm not. They told me they'd found a trail of fluid, which makes it very simple. But what you don't know, Lisette, is that Clarke, Eugene's chauffeur, is a marvel with cars. Before, when Eugene still felt I was precious to him, he never let me take out the car without Clarke checking it. Suppose when Clarke was checking it, the hose was loosened, so that it would come away—no, you couldn't believe that, could you? It wouldn't make sense to you."

Her voice was growing increasingly high-pitched. I said, "It would make sense, Irene, if someone wanted to kill you. But isn't it possible that you're becoming neurotic?—"

"Yes, I'm becoming neurotic. Eugene will want you to believe that. He'll probably tell you I've had a whiplash that has upset my nervous system, something as logical as that. And so I need pills to sleep. And I imagine things, such as Clarke unloosening that hose so I should lose control of the car!" She laughed wildly. "And the stomach upsets, too, they're quite natural. People in that part of the world always get some bug in their system, call it the amoeba, or food poisoning. That's what they said when I went to the hospital for them."

I said carefully, "Are you suggesting you were poisoned, Irene? They must have taken analyses."

"I responded to treatment," she said. "It may not have been thought necessary to take analyses. Mid-East hospitals aren't as thorough as ours."

I was silent.

"Your face is so transparent, Lisette. I can read your mind. Irene is neurotic, unhappy over losing her husband's love, taking too many sleeping pills, getting sick, having fancies. Maybe she *did* have a whiplash, maybe it *did* throw her off balance, maybe she *is* mad."

"I don't think that—"

"You're not very convincing, Lisette. But let me ask you this: have you ever awakened from sleep and seen some monstrous creature holding a knife to your throat?"

"I've had nightmares—"

She disregarded me, hurrying on, her eyes wide and staring, "In our house in Teheran the windows were barred, and the stone walls outside were rimmed with broken bottles. A barbarous custom, to repel housebreakers." She shuddered. "Eugene was away, but said he would be back late. I'd left a light burning in my dressing room. That was how I saw its face. He had a rubber mask over it, I suppose, but it was horrible. I felt the touch of his knife on my throat, and then it cut me, and I seemed to wake, and scream, and scream, and he ran away."

I took a breath. "You have all that jewelry."

72

"He didn't take any."

"You frightened him away before he did."

"Eugene said that, too. But you see, I didn't imagine him. He did get away over the wall, but he left blood there, on the broken glass."

"These things do happen, Irene. A rich house, among so many poor—"

"Believe what you want," she said despairingly. "But I think Eugene hired that man. Maybe not to kill me, that would be too quick, but to cut me and disfigure me, so I would be ugly for the rest of my life."

It was a shocking idea, and for a minute I could hardly answer her. Could it be true? It was fantastic and incredible, but I had learned bitterly how nothing was too fantastic, nothing too incredible. I tried to think reasonably, as much for my sake as for hers. "I don't see why he wouldn't choose to divorce you, rather than risk being exposed as endangering your life. He is an important man, you said so yourself. He has more than enough grounds for divorce, and he would probably win. Wouldn't that be simpler than risking his position, his status, everything?"

"You don't understand, Lisette. He won't risk anything. Whatever he does will be carefully worked out so as not to endanger him."

"But I'm here. Jim's here. He knows you will confide in me, at least, if not in Jim."

"Maybe he's confident that you will think I'm unbalanced. As you do," she said quietly.

"But still, why should he be so insanely vindictive?"

"Eugene's feelings toward me were never moderate.

He loved to an almost insane degree. He hates in the same way. Oh, he conceals it. You'd never guess it on the surface. He is bent on hurting me as much as I hurt him."

I could only stare at her now, wordless.

"It's why he's chosen this house, this place. There's no one for miles to see, to wonder. Maybe he will even drive me to suicide, maybe that's his intention, to make me so miserable I'll kill myself. And there are times when I want to, Lisette, when I think I will."

I cried out, "Then why do you stay with him?" I should have asked her before; I suppose I was too disturbed by her story to think clearly. "He can't keep you if you want to go, can he? We're here to help you—he wouldn't stop you with us here!"

Her laugh caught and smothered in her throat. "Yes, he might let me go, with you here. But I can't. I won't."

I waited, bewildered.

"I'm still in love with him."

"But Irene—"

"Yes. Call me a lunatic. Or a masochist. Or both. But there it is. I love him. I want to believe he will love me again some day. That this insane anger against me will die, and what he once felt for me will come back."

I could only say, "You're not thinking clearly, Irene. If you believe he is out to hurt you, if he is unbalanced, you're in serious danger *now*."

"I'm prepared to take the risk. It's why I've stayed with him through all this."

Her manner was suddenly quiet; I could almost believe she knew what she was doing, that her words were thought out and conclusive. It was easier to reason with

74

her wild accusations than this sober conviction. I said troubledly, "You know what Uncle Willy would do if he were here? He'd snatch you away on the first plane out. He'd blame me for not doing the same thing, if he knew."

"Lisette, he's not to know! Not my father! Not Aunt Beck! You understand? They're not to know any of this!"

She put both hands on my arms and almost shook me with her intensity.

"I won't leave him! No matter what you or anyone says! Not while there's a chance for us! I'm gambling with my life, and I don't care, because if I lost him, nothing would matter anymore. Do you understand that, Lisette?"

What could I say? I was helpless in the face of her passion. And I did not know what to believe, I did not know enough about Eugene, or Irene as she was, to be able to winnow out the truth from what she told me. Even if there was a shred of veracity to her words, I felt she should not stay here, but how could I make her go, feeling as she did?

"You promise not to say anything, Lisette? Promise?"

I had to promise. She sank back on the sofa, exhausted by her outburst, and I watched her unhappily. After a while she seemed to rouse herself.

"I've been selfish as usual, talking about my problems, not even asking you about yours, about Dan."

"It's all right, Irene."

"You must want to go to your room. I haven't even let you do that."

"I didn't mind. I wanted to hear about you."

"It's dismal, isn't it? It was selfish of me to plunge you

75

into it, but you can't imagine how much I wanted you here, how glad I am you are here."

She was almost her old self as we went up the stairs, as if she had purged herself of a poison and was well again.

"I hope you don't mind Jim being here. I cast around desperately for someone who might be good company for you when you want to get away from Eugene and me, and luckily he could come. He's a cousin of Eugene's, and I thought I could get Eugene to agree to inviting another guest more easily if it were a relative of his."

I had been right, then, in sensing that Eugene hadn't wanted us, that it was not his choice that we were here. Why, unless it suited his purposes to have Irene alone?

❧ 6

*M*y room at Skeld House was square and bleak, due mainly to rough whitewashed walls on which the cold north light shone through plain starched white curtains. At night, I discovered, when Gerda laid the fires, the room changed its character. The heavy draperies were drawn even now in July, the bed was plump with a quilted comforter, and the bathroom beyond was new and tiled in pink.

There was a spareness to most of the house that surprised me, but then I was to learn that this was Scotland, not England, and not even the mainland of Scotland but an island, to which luxuries came less prodigally. Irene might have warmed it with her own things, but since they had leased Skeld House only until October, she may not have thought it worthwhile. She had never been too interested in houses, or housekeeping. The only apartment she'd ever rented had been after she'd begun making her own money as a model, and a decorator friend had done it for her. I remember it as a perfect setting for her, as if her friend had understood her well. It was always full of fresh flowers, and there was yellow-painted furniture, and a lovely green carpet like grass underfoot. It was always too hot, like a greenhouse. Irene did not belong in the austere setting of this house; what was painful to me was that she seemed resigned, as if she hadn't the heart or the energy to change it.

We lunched in a somber dining room, with heavy silver dishes on the sideboard, on a cloth of plain white linen.

Irene shrugged. "Everything came with the house."

It wasn't a large house. Downstairs, besides the drawing room and the dining room, there was only a library, where a television set stood incongruously on a fine Jacobean oak table. We did not stop to see the kitchen and pantries. "They're *her* place," she said, meaning Mrs. Wall.

Upstairs, too, there were surprisingly few rooms. Jim had the bedroom opposite mine; I could see Jarvie in it, unpacking Jim's luggage. Gerda had already put away my things on hangers and in drawers, even setting out the photograph of Dan that I'd brought along.

Irene's room was at the far end of the hall. It was almost as large as the drawing room, and the most elaborately furnished, with armoires of massive oak and a square canopy draped in brocade framing her bed. I ran my hand over a fur blanket.

She said wryly, "It's cold, sleeping alone."

Her room connected to Eugene's through a pair of doors. Hers stood open, his was locked; she showed that to me pointedly. To see Eugene's room we had to use the hall door, which was open. His room was small, even smaller than mine, and held a single bed and a desk, with a book open and face down on it.

Irene flicked the pages. "He reads a lot these nights," she said almost musingly. Before she closed the door behind us she turned and studied the room, as if it held some mystery.

"Do the servants sleep in the house?"

"Just Mrs. Wall and Gerda, on the floor above. Clarke and Jarvie and the gardener have an apartment over the garage. Only the cook goes home at night after dinner. Her husband works in the freezer plant down the coast, and their cottage is within biking distance. She used to be cook at the hotel, and does all kinds of puddings." She shuddered. "We couldn't get our cook in Teheran to come, and no wonder. Anyway, I really don't care. Food disgusts me these days."

I remember her hanging around the kitchen in my mother's house whenever she came to visit. I remember how she used to enjoy sampling whatever Bertha prepared.

We came out again into the cold, sparsely furnished hall. I said, "It isn't raining now. Let's go for a walk."

"If you want. I won't go very far. I do seem to get tired easily, but it will probably start to rain soon, anyway."

It seemed warmer outdoors than in, as if the thick walls retained the cold and the dampness. The sun came out fitfully, and a soft, salty wind blew without letup. I stopped to admire the hardy flowers struggling in their symmetrical beds.

"I'd prefer a heated pool instead."

"Can you bathe in the ocean?"

She shivered, "If it ever gets to be summer up here."

There were horses in the stables, she pointed out, if I wanted to ride, and the garage held a number of small cars that looked like jeeps but were Land Rovers. The greenhouse, large and workmanlike, provided flowers as well as vegetables.

Once past the outbuildings and the walls, emptiness took over abruptly: now there was only earth and sky. The impact of utter silence is indescribable; I felt overwhelmed.

She said, "Would you like to talk about Dan?"

Strange that it should be easy to talk in this void, far from the familiar world that had once sheltered me, under a gray and indifferent sky. The closeness between Irene and me had not been ruptured by the years of separation since her marriage. I had once thought of her as my older sister; it was still the same. Most of the time I was able to talk casually about Dan, but now and then my voice failed, and then she would put her arm through mine and murmur, poor Lisette, I know how awful it must have been, how unbearable, all the conventional phrases of sympathy, but which, from Irene, were more than that to me, and comforting. I think, too, I was beginning to sense the change that had already begun to take place, the scar tissue forming, sealing over the raw places. He was dead, and I was alive. I could face it.

I talked myself dry. Then she started on small talk, about my mother and did she still use Mary Chess in her bureau drawers, about her father who had never remarried even though he mentioned in his letters a succession of nice, *suitable* women, as Irene put it. "My mother was never for Daddy," she said. "He should have seen it, so he wouldn't have been so shocked when she left him. He's good, and darling, but a bore." She saw my expression. "Look, Lisette, face it. He and Aunt Beck are so alike. Can you imagine either of them having sex? Wanting someone passionately? Being passionately desired?"

"It's because they're our parents."

"No, sweetie, it's more."

We walked on. She said suddenly, "Do you like Jim?"

"Very much. I'm glad he's here."

"Isn't he the most attractive man?"

I hugged her arm against me. "Please don't dream up any romance for me, Irene. Not yet. I'm not ready."

"Of course not. It's too soon. And yet," she said, "it's what would help you the most, having someone tell you you're pretty, and that he wants you."

"And you? Maybe it would be the best thing for you, too." I spoke tentatively, afraid to depress her. "A clean break. Starting in all over again, forgetting the past."

"I won't believe it's hopeless. It can't be. It mustn't be."

The North Sea appeared below us, the land sloping steeply down to meet it. Flat rocks outlined the shore, gleaming sleekly where the water washed over them.

"Eugene said there were seals."

We found them, as sleekly brown as the rocks and almost indistinguishable from them except when they slithered about or flopped into the water.

Irene was restless. "Look, we'll be caught in the rain."

I hadn't noticed the darkening sky. We weren't caught in the rain, though the mist was as dense as rain, but the gray sedan was already in front of the door when we reached the house. Irene went up to her room at once; I looked into the drawing room and found Jim.

"What a climate," he said. "Now I know how they came to invent Scotch here." He was opening cupboard doors. "They seem to have hidden the whiskey." He located a tapestry bell-pull and rang for Jarvie.

"Scotch okay with you, Lisette?"

I nodded, kicking off my sodden shoes and stretching my damp feet toward the fire. Jarvie returned with the tray, and Jim fixed my drink and his own.

My head was too preoccupied with the story Irene had told me for me to attempt to talk about anything else. "Jim, how long has Irene been—" I hesitated; how to put it?—ill? frightened? neurotic? I finished, "—like this?"

"You mean, the way she looks?" He frowned. "I can't say for sure. As I told you, I was hardly an intimate of theirs. She did have an accident with the car and seemed to go downhill after that. She was in and out of the hospital a few times, and the talk was that she had some bug. Intestinal."

The door opened, and Jim looked up.

"Here's Eugene. Why don't you ask him?"

"Ask me what?" he said. He had changed into a dark suit and white shirt, against which his face looked wind-burned. I was beginning to see him through Irene's eyes now, which was unfair, perhaps, as someone who was bitter, confiding in no one, brooding over thoughts of retribution.

"Irene never wrote that she was sick," I said. "Uncle Willy said you had said she was tired and tense, but we had no idea it was anything serious."

"Is it serious?" He raised his eyebrows.

I felt somehow he was making fun of me.

"I didn't know it was serious," he said. "The doctors say there's nothing organically wrong with her."

"It could be emotional. Or psychological."

"I'm afraid I don't know any more than the doctors." He spoke with finality, as if he wanted to end my questions.

I wouldn't be put off. "She looks shocking. There must be something someone can do."

"If the doctors had thought so, they would have kept her in a hospital by force."

It seemed incredible that he should be talking of his wife in this detached way.

"You haven't seen her in a few years," he said. "She's older, remember, and she's been living a very fast life."

"It has to be more than that, Gene," Jim said.

Eugene hesitated. "She may need psychiatric care."

I was taken aback. "But how can she get that here?"

Again he seemed to hesitate. "She already started with some good men, and then dropped them. There was even a fine clinic in London, but she refused to stay. Quite frankly, I've given up. She refuses to go on."

"Given up!" I cried. I stopped. I said, "Do you think

83

this is the environment she needs?" I tried to go on calmly.

"The medical consensus was that since she's rejected outside help, the best benefit might come from complete quiet, complete rest, fresh air, and sleep. She has all of that here."

I said, "Why do you think she needs psychiatric help?"

"Have you a better theory?"

I heard the dry warning, but I went on, "Was it in her mind when that man broke in and slashed her?"

Jim looked stunned; he turned to Eugene.

Eugene was under too complete control for me to guess if I had made him uncomfortable.

He said, with deliberation, "No, that wasn't in her mind. Someone did break into her room. What was in her mind, I think, was why he was there. She imagines he came to attack her. I believe it's more likely he was after her jewelry. If he held a knife to her, it was probably to frighten her into silence. He was caught a few weeks later and admitted to breaking into several houses in our neighborhood."

"Hell, even so," Jim said, "that could be a shattering experience to someone in a lot sounder condition than Irene was after her accident. Haven't the doctors suggested that she's having a kind of nervous breakdown?"

"No, but if you find it a convenient term, you can call it that."

I stood up. I couldn't bear his evident lack of concern, or his irony at ours. "I'm going to change."

As I left I heard Jim begin to make conversation

about the quality of the Scotch in Scotland. Irene had been right at least in this: if it ever came to a choice of credibility, it would be Eugene who would be believed. The groundwork had been laid deftly. Irene's trouble was in her mind; it was Jim not Eugene who had suggested the possibility of a nervous breakdown. Eugene had already mentioned her visits to psychiatrists, time spent in clinics, all pointing to an emotional disorder. I might have believed Eugene myself, if I hadn't heard Irene's story.

I forced myself out of a comforting hot bath, reluctant to face the tensions when we four met again, but there was no way to avoid it. I dressed and went down.

Irene called to me from the head of the stairs to wait for her. She had changed into some caftanlike outfit, over which she wore Eastern jewelry of gold and pearls. It seemed an extravagant way to dress for a dinner at Skeld House.

She read my expression. "I know, I'm all decked out. Please don't mind. I have to distract people from my face, and besides, one of the few pleasures left to me is dressing up. All the lovely things I have—pointless now." She lifted her shoulders and let them fall. "I dream. Maybe Gene will remember how he felt when he bought me these things. I'm a fool."

We'd all had our drinks earlier and Irene did not want any, so we went directly to the dining room. It looked more festive now, with the chandelier lit and its hundreds of crystal prisms shedding a tremulous light on fresh roses from their greenhouse, but in spite of that and Irene's splendor, the atmosphere was forced and oppressive. Jarvie served, with Gerda; Mrs. Wall did not appear. Jim drank several glasses of wine to dissipate the mood, but his attempts at light talk fell flat. I asked questions, and they were answered, and then silence again. I thought of the countless meals like this that lay ahead, and my heart sank.

Irene pushed food around with her fork, but hardly any of it reached her mouth. She didn't speak to Eugene, or he to her. I don't know why she should have brought up the notes, unless, like us, she was only trying to make conversation.

"Whatever happened to those missing notes, Lisette? I gathered they're causing Daddy a lot of anguish."

I had anticipated, with Jim, that there would be talk even here in Skeld House about the notes, but I hadn't expected it so soon, maybe because at this moment they were very far from my mind. Dismayed, I could only sit for a moment, open-mouthed, wondering what I could say. Even more disconcerting, Eugene had turned on me an intent and oddly searching glance.

He said, "I saw your mother's letter to Irene. I'd like to hear your version of what happened."

I was a guest in his house. To say that it was my own affair and I preferred not to talk about it seemed rude, in view of the fact that my mother's relentless letter-writing had probably left nothing secret. Unhappily, I went through the story again, in as objective and unimpassioned a manner as I could. I finished with, "And that's all there is to it."

Eugene's eyes had never left me as I talked. Now he

said, very much the way Jim had, "Why do they believe you may have taken them?"

"I don't think they believe that anymore," I said defiantly. "They did allow me to leave the country. They thought it was an accident, and they searched my apartment to see if I might have put them away without thinking."

"Why *did* you leave your job?" he said.

I resented his question. "I preferred not to work there anymore."

Jim said, "Face it, Eugene, she's not cut out to be a Mata Hari. She'd need another twenty pounds for that."

"It's so utterly ridiculous," Irene said. "How could they take it seriously?"

Eugene said briefly, "Because it *is* serious."

"I don't want to think about them anymore," I said, with a brave show of firmness. "My connection with the notes is finished."

"Have you thought that your coming here might be considered suspicious?" he said.

"Will you stop, Eugene!" Irene said. "If I'd known you were going to fasten onto it this way, I'd never have brought it up."

He said, "I think it's important that Lisette understand her position. Whoever it is that has found out that she's connected with the notes, and someone has, because Lisette believes her apartment had a going over, and not by the FBI, whoever it is probably also knows where she is now. It's an ideal spot to make contact, out of the way, she's likely to be unobserved—"

"Like in the movies," I said tightly. "A lonely rendez-

87

vous along the coast, the enemy agent would arrive by boat, maybe submarine, with a winking lantern for a signal—"

He said, "You're treating it rather lightly. The whole affair seems to have been handled with the most careless security. To have allowed you to leave the building without first searching your handbag—"

"The guard knew me! I worked there three years, I was highly trusted!"

"You can't be sure, ever," he said. "Emotions are tricky. They're a lot more persuasive than intelligence."

Irene cried, "He thinks women are all immoral and weak!"

"I didn't say that."

"But you believe it! You know you do!"

He didn't raise his voice. "I don't think women are any more weak or immoral than men. I don't think they're governed by their emotions any more than men are. I think there are women who are hardheaded and calculating just as I know there are men who succumb to passion. We're not discussing that right now, Irene. I'm only commenting on the general lack of care. The office security. Lisette's carelessness."

"I'm not considered a careless person," I said. "I'm considered very conscientious. Usually."

"Then it was out of character for you to mislay those notes. And a good reason for them to suspect you."

"Eugene, I asked you to stop," Irene said.

"I don't see why this can't be brought out in the open."

"Because Lisette is our guest, and you're making her unhappy! You're doing it deliberately! I know you are! I won't stay here and listen to any more!" She rose, pushing back her chair so abruptly that it crashed to the floor. She ran to the stairs.

I was full of consternation, not only because of the talk of the notes and my part in their loss and the feeling that Eugene did not completely accept my innocence, but because I'd precipitated this scene between Eugene and Irene.

He stood up and righted the chair, but gave no other sign that he was affected by Irene's behavior. "I didn't intend to upset you, Lisette. I thought a discussion might even jog your memory, in case you had mislaid them."

I couldn't even bring myself to answer.

"Look, can we drop it for now?" Jim said. "It isn't getting anywhere, and it's just making Lisette unhappy."

We retreated to the drawing room for coffee. Irene did not come down again, and the first moment I could find to break away, I went up to her room to look for her.

She was sitting on the edge of her bed, her face taut.

"I'm sorry, Irene. I wish it hadn't come up. I wish it hadn't created a scene between you and Eugene. You don't have to defend me against him. I can handle it myself."

"You didn't see what he was trying to do. I did."

"He just wanted me to realize the position I was in. As if I didn't already."

"He wants you to feel unwelcome here. That's his purpose. If he's unpleasant enough, you might leave. And Jim with you. The only reason Jim is here is because of you."

"But why, Irene? If he's out to prove you're nervous

and neurotic, as you say he is, he should want people here, so he can convince them."

"But he won't convince you, and he knows that. He knows I've told you the way things really are."

I hesitated. There was some logic to what she said.

She caught my hands. "Lisette, he won't convince you, will he?"

"Of course not."

"And you'll stay, no matter what?"

I promised that, too.

She seemed relieved, but only for the moment. She whispered, "Do you think he hates me?"

I said honestly, "I don't know. I'd say he's sort of cold and detached. Not just toward you. Toward all of us." I couldn't tell her I found him indifferent to her, unconcerned about her; it would be too cruel.

"His mind is always planning," she said. "I never did feel I knew him. But he can be very charming and very persuasive. You'll want to believe him. He's very strong. I never was able to reach him, except through sex. But women find that strength exciting in a man. And Lisette, if he senses you don't trust him, he'll do everything to bring you around."

The drafts stirred the heavy drapes even though the windows were closed. She shivered.

"I hate the nights worst of all. And the fire is too far away to warm this large room."

"Irene, come downstairs and have coffee with us. You look so beautiful in that dress, it's a shame to waste it."

She shook her head. "I feel jittery. It hurts me to be

with him, see his coldness. I'll go to bed. It's warm, at least, in bed."

I turned away, filled with pity, afraid she would see it.

"Lisette, he'll twist everything to suit himself. He'll make it all so credible. You won't believe him?"

"I promised you I wouldn't."

She drew a long breath. "I'm sorry it has to be this way. I wish it could be happier here, for your sake. At least there's Jim. He'll try to make things pleasant."

When I went downstairs, I found only Jim in the drawing room.

"Eugene went out. I've been waiting to have my second cup of coffee with you."

We settled ourselves comfortably in front of the fire. He said, "If I brought out a pipe, would you think it's just a ploy to make myself irresistible?" I laughed, and he said ruefully, "I bought one to help me quit cigarettes. Now I smoke both."

For an attractive man, he was entirely unselfconscious. Irene had been like that, once, wearing her beauty like a comfortable dress, heedless of it. Conversation was easy. I found myself telling him about my mother's hangups and how much happier I'd been since I lived alone. I told him about Dan. I tried to describe how I'd always thought of Irene, unfettered, dazzling, destined for some exciting future. I had to insist that we turn the talk to him. He told me about his father's invention and how he should have been a millionaire from it, but he had worked on it when he was with Atico, and there was something about its belonging to them because he had done it on their time.

"Not that they weren't generous. They were. But my father sank most of what they paid to him back into other inventions, none of them paying off. I'm afraid if I want the good life, I'll have to work for it. I'm not as lucky as Eugene. Still, I've always admired Eugene. He's done a lot for the company."

"Is that the only reason you admire him?"

He grinned. "I'd admire him more if he recognized my ability, which he hasn't." He said more soberly, "I can't say I like the way he handles Irene. In his place, I'd show a little more sympathy."

I thought he would, too. "Do you have a girl?" I asked.

He grinned again. "Whenever I can. Actually, there's no one special at the moment. I was seriously involved for a while, but she wouldn't marry me. I didn't have enough money. She wanted a rich man, she was beautiful, and she got him. Like Irene."

"Irene didn't want just any rich man, I'm sure. She's in love with Eugene."

"I always thought so. And he with her," he said. "But something's up between them that's not quite right. There'd been some gossip in Teheran, but then, well, men have always admired Irene, and people out there have nothing much to do but talk. I'm sure there'd be nobody to take Eugene's place with Irene."

I agreed.

He said, "In a way, the change in him is almost as pronounced as it is in Irene. Maybe it's just the strain of her illness, but I have a hunch it's something more. He's unfriendly, don't you feel that? If it had been just me, I'd have said, well, he doesn't like being reminded that he owes me something, but he's the same with you."

At least Jim would survey the situation here with an unbiased mind. I had been afraid he might be influenced by Eugene's position, and his need to ingratiate himself, so that he might shut his eyes to the true state of affairs.

When we stood up to say goodnight, I found myself unwilling to go right up to bed. I wanted some fresh air, even for a moment, and I went to the entry for my coat.

"Going out?"

"Just to clear my head. Sitting in front of the fire so long, I feel as if I've swallowed smoke."

"Me too," he said. "I'll come with you."

Even now there was a faint turquoise light in the sky, like an advanced dusk. And again that encompassing stillness. We left the door open, because neither of us had a key and the servants had gone to bed, and we walked across the lawn to the road. Our feet made no sound on the wet earth. We were silent, too, as if to appreciate the stillness of the night. Maybe we had simply talked ourselves out. We walked arm in arm, taking gulps of the frosty, damp air. At the road I yawned.

"Me too," he said. "Let's go back."

It was because of the silence that their low voices carried. They must have been behind one of the sheds, invisible to us, as we were invisible to them. All we heard was the low, indistinguishable murmur, two voices, one of them Eugene's.

Jim lifted his eyebrows. We paused for an instant, as if we might recognize whom Eugene was talking to. Even as we paused, the voices stopped. A man's figure crossed the driveway, his back to us, a short, heavily built man. That was all I could see, except that he was completely bald, his bare scalp almost luminous in the dusky light. He disappeared behind the outbuildings.

We continued on to the house.

"Must be one of the servants," Jim said, as we hung up our raincoats.

Eugene came in as we reached the stairs.

"Still up?" Eugene said.

"We went out for some air."

Pause.

"Just now?" Eugene said.

He seemed to speak very carefully.

"We came in only a minute or two before you did," Jim said, surprised. I wondered if he were surprised by Eugene's question. "In fact, we heard you talking to someone, but we didn't want to interrupt."

Eugene still spoke carefully. "Talking to someone?"

"Yes. Over near one of the sheds."

Pause. Hardly perceptible this time. "Oh, yes. Clarke. He didn't feel like sleeping either. He can't get used to the midnight sun. Well, I'm for bed, too."

We went upstairs together, separating at our different doors. Eugene's door had hardly closed behind him when Jim caught me before I closed mine.

"Now that was odd," he said.

"What was?"

"I know Clarke. He's the chauffeur, been with Eugene for years. He's got a head of reddish hair. I could swear the man outside was bald."

94

"He was."

He looked at me, shrugged. "Odd," he said again, and went back to his room.

If it wasn't Clarke, why had Eugene lied?

❧ 7

*T*he question was still in my mind when I awoke: why had he lied? If it was a lie. But the more I thought of his actions of the night before, the surer I was that he had been disconcerted by the possibility that we had overheard his conversation or seen the man he had been with.

Jim must have been mulling over the same thoughts and coming to the same conclusion. He, too, had slept late and was just starting his breakfast when I came down. Irene was there, keeping us company and drinking black coffee. His conversation was pointed at getting information from Irene.

"You've been pretty lucky with your staff," he said. "You've had them with you for years."

"You mean Mrs. Wall? You couldn't pry her away from Eugene with a crowbar."

I glanced over my shoulder, afraid Mrs. Wall might be in the room.

"What about Clarke?"

"Oh, Clarke is closer to Eugene than some of his

business associates. He was Eugene's driver in the Army, you know. They're practically buddies."

"Are they the only two that stayed with you?"

She nodded. "Jarvie and the gardener Nichols came with the house. Jarvie engaged the cook and Gerda. I suspect that the only thing that keeps Gerda here is that there's something going between her and Clarke."

"He's a good-looking guy," Jim said. "He has red hair, doesn't he?" He looked at her.

"Last time I noticed, he did." She lifted her brows. "What makes you interested in Clarke's hair?"

We had to laugh, and Jim was able to go on smoothly, "I wondered when I got your invitation how you were going to manage without that army of help you had in Teheran. But you seem to be doing all right."

"We don't live on the same scale here, obviously. We don't entertain at all. Remember our gardens there, and the men necessary to keep them up? There's nothing here, hardly. Nichols handles it himself, except for some help now and then from his twelve-year-old grandson."

The man we'd seen could have been someone from Atico. But after midnight? And why wouldn't Eugene have said so?

The day turned fine, soft, and humid, and uncharacteristically windless. Jim suggested we go riding. At first Irene shook her head. "You two go."

"You always rode so well, Irene."

She must have been hungry for even that crumb of admiration from Jim; she hesitated, and then agreed. When we met in the hall she wore handsomely cut riding pants and a cashmere sweater, and her fair hair was carefully bound up in a scarf. I thought it an encouraging sign that she came out with us, no matter what the reason.

Clarke was polishing the car outside the garage; he had red hair, a thatch of it. He went along with us to the stable to saddle the horses for us and help us onto them. It was at least ten years since summer camp, when I'd last gone riding, and I was unsteady at first, but Irene and Jim were considerate and went slowly until I could get accustomed to the gait of the horse. Gradually, all the lessons I'd had in camp came back to me, and I was able to keep up with them when they went more briskly. Irene did ride beautifully; I was lost in admiration for her, as I'd always been when I was growing up. There had never been any competition between us, maybe because she was eight years older and simply too far above me in every way. I knew I must seem awkward beside her, in my jeans and sneakers, clutching the reins too stiffly, but I didn't mind, giving myself up to the pleasure of riding.

It was easy going over the low grass. Sometimes we followed a path that could once have led to a crofter's cottage or a fisherman's hut, but mostly it was over open fields. I discovered an oddly shaped hump, overgrown with grass, and pointed. "What's that?"

"That's our *broch*," Irene said.

We rode up to it and dismounted. Jim fastened the bridles to some stones, and the horses nibbled at the mossy grass while we wandered among the two concentric rings of stones standing up like a wall around the *broch*. They reminded me of a mouth with most of the teeth gone; the stones that remained must have been too deeply embedded to be dug up.

The doorway into the *broch* was so low that even I had to stoop to enter. We found ourselves in a round chamber lined with stones, the lower part of what must once have been a tower, and were silent for some moments, overwhelmed by its awesome age.

"We should have brought a flash," Jim said.

Earth and grass had grown over the sides and top of the truncated tower, so that no light came in except through the low doorway. But I was becoming used to the darkness, and now I could even make out a series of cells hollowed out in its walls.

"I wonder what they made these for."

"Some of them were used as bedrooms," Irene said. "At least that's what the man from Edinburgh told us when he was here. I can only think that the people then must have been a lot smaller than they are now."

Jim was peering into one. "It almost seems as if there were steps here. I'll bet they went up to the top of the tower."

There seemed to have been apertures once, but the stones had settled, and the earth filled in the cracks. Some of the cells were barred by slabs of rock that fitted over them like doors.

"They must have used them to store things inside, maybe even treasure, stuff they wanted to keep hidden," Jim said.

He tried to move one of the slabs by rocking it back and forth in the earth, but he could budge it only a trifle.

My feet were already numb with cold. "How could they bear it?"

"They probably kept a fire going here in the middle.

The smoke could rise out of the top of the tower, and they could lie in those little cells and watch it. Cozy," Jim said.

"*Cozy,*" Irene said. "It's like an open grave."

It was as cold as a grave, and musty, smelling of damp earth. Suddenly I wanted only to get out into the sunlight. I hurried toward the doorway, as if someone or something might block it before we could get through.

"We'll all get pneumonia," Irene said, following. She turned her pale face upward. "How do people live without sun!"

Maybe because of the contrast with that dank place and its smell of dead centuries, the moor seemed suddenly splendid, high and windswept and beautiful. We mounted and rode fast, as if to get the feel of the *broch* out of us. Now and then we'd come upon the sea, wide and glittering like silk. I felt exhilarated all at once, glad to be alive. It had been a long time since I'd felt this way; I'd wondered if I ever would again. Now I knew it was possible.

We were circling back to the house. It was already in sight on its knob of land, starkly white, bristling with chimneys. Even as we neared it, we saw a figure emerge from the back door, mount a bicycle, and pedal off.

"It's Mrs. Wall," said Irene. "Now where would she be going in that direction?"

"What's in that direction?" Jim said.

"Nothing. Absolutely nothing."

"Maybe you ought to try and get her attention," I said. "Maybe she's looking for us."

"Let her look, then," Irene said darkly.

"She has something in the basket." I could see the

basket behind her covered with a white cloth of some kind. "Could she be bringing us lunch? Maybe she thinks the weather is good enough for a picnic."

"Or she's fixed a little special tidbit for Eugene," Irene said. "I wonder why he'd meet her out there?"

"Maybe the old girl just wants some sunshine, too," Jim said. "Why don't you forget about her?"

Mrs. Wall was already out of sight, so we couldn't have called her back if we tried. We rode up to the stables. Clarke wasn't around, so Jim helped us down and led off the horses. He had hugged me briefly when I dismounted; I wouldn't have noted it, it was so casual, but I felt Irene's eyes on us. They were contemplative, almost wistful. I thought, let her believe what it pleases her to believe; I didn't mind.

Mrs. Wall was back to serve lunch, so she couldn't have gone very far or stayed very long. Her bicycle leaned under the kitchen window when I passed it, and the basket was empty. It seemed incredible that there should be someone out there whom she had gone to meet, and yet the thought fell like a chilling shadow.

But after that first week the days began to move quickly and uneventfully. I forgot about the bald man, and Mrs. Wall's errand, and even if there was some relation. We discovered a meticulously clipped grass court, and on good days Jim and I played tennis. Irene watched, even languidly tossing back balls that rolled near her. On the days when we didn't walk, Jim drove one of the Land Rovers to the ruined castle in Scalloway, or to the Viking settlement in Jarlshof. There were caves to visit and pierced rocks standing out of the sea like giant stabiles.

We grew to know every solitary cottage—the one with geraniums in a lard tub beside the door, the one with dazzling hollyhocks leaning through the missing pickets of a wind-downed fence. We saw the earliest of the heather opening, like a mauve mist over the slopes.

I rarely saw Eugene until dinner. Irene would sweep down in some striking costume that seemed to ask that he notice her, the lamplight softening her worn face with the occasional spot of color in her cheeks, jewels winking in her ears, on her wrists and fingers. But he barely acknowledged her presence except in the most formal of courtesies, such as seating her or handing her a coffee cup. She made an effort to ignore his implacable indifference, but sometimes it was plainly more than she could bear. That night of the Coast Guard Ball, for instance.

Jim brought it up almost as a joke. He read the local paper whenever it was delivered with the groceries, and he announced at dinner: "The Coast Guard is having its annual ball at the Lerwick Hotel."

"They sent an invitation to the office," Eugene said. "You're invited, if you care to go."

"How about it?" Jim said. "Absorb some local color? Have a dance or two?"

Irene's face became animated. "I haven't danced in ages!" She looked at Eugene. "Why don't we go! It would be fun for Lisette and Jim."

A long look passed between them. I did not understand it, I only knew that Irene turned away first, her face taut, trying for control.

Jim had seen the look, too. He frowned slightly, and then he said, "How about it, Gene?"

"Go, if you want," Eugene said. "I can't, I have some reports to go over, but Irene can go with you if she wants."

There was an uncomfortable silence. Irene said, shrillness creeping into her voice, "It wouldn't be much fun for Jim and Lisette if I tagged along without you."

"I'm sorry, Irene, but I can't go." He did not look at her.

"Don't worry about coming with us, Irene," Jim said quickly. "I can handle two women easily."

"You're making a point, Eugene," she said. "You want to humiliate me in front of them."

"You're being melodramatic," he said. "I have some work to do, that's all."

Her voice rose, thinning: "You know there isn't anything you have to do that can't wait another day! You purposely encouraged them about the dance so you could show them that you will not be seen with me!"

Eugene put down his coffee cup and left the room.

She stared after him and then burst into hysterical weeping. Jim brought her water, I held her and patted her until she quieted down. Nothing was further from my mind by now than going to the dance, but when it seemed as if we would all stay home with her, she grew feverishly insistent.

"You're only staying home because of us! You're making me feel worse! Please go! I want you to go!"

In the end it seemed simpler to go. We went reluctantly, as if it were a duty we were being forced to do, but as we drove toward Lerwick, we gradually found ourselves distracted by the loveliness of the evening and slowly permitted it to seduce us. There was a violet light in the air, and the gray-green moor was streaked with that special flush of sunset you only see near water. Only the sound of our motor broke the stillness, and except for the inevitable sheep trotting along the side of the road every now and then, hobnobbing like old friends shoulder to shoulder, their eyes as shiny as bakelite in the car's headlights, we saw no other living creature.

Lerwick seemed like a city after the quiet of our countryside. It seemed strange to see young men clustering in the square near the harbor, to see streetlamps and the lights swinging from the masts of the fishing boats. I looked for the *St. Clere*, but she would not be back until Wednesday morning.

"I haven't really explored Lerwick," I said. "I'd like to drive down some time during the day, when the shops are open."

"Let's do it together," Jim said. "Feels great to get away, doesn't it? It's cruel to say, but I'm a little fed up with our oil tycoon and his glamorous wife. This is the first free breath I've drawn in weeks."

I had to agree with him.

We found the new hotel on the Scalloway Road; it was a low, modern building more like a motel, still not finished, with painters' ladders leaning against one wing. But there were what seemed like dozens of small cars lining its circular drive, so that we had to park some distance away. Behind the hotel the land was raw and untouched, sprinkled with wild flowers, sloping to the sea, which was stained a deep purple by what was left of the twilight.

Even as we walked up, the hotel seemed to shake with the thump of dancers. The ball was in the dining room, the music was loud, with a resounding beat, and already the air was thick with smoke and overheated. The floor was jammed, the coastguardsmen a solid lot, bearded, some of them, dressed in neat dark suits, their wives dressed in crepe and with hairdos obviously just released from rollers and pincurls. Those who weren't dancing lined up at a buffet that stretched the length of the room and held platters of turkey and ham and roast beef and whole, jellied fish. Beer was being poured frothing from a barrel behind the bar.

Jim managed the introductions, and we were invited to sit at a table beside the dance floor. The music was too loud for talk; we shouted a few words back and forth, but mostly we danced. Now and then Jim would drop a kiss on my hair or my forehead; I didn't mind, I rather liked it. I rather liked him, I thought. I liked being held in his arms, I liked his liking me.

We drove home lightheaded from the beer, singing the outdated songs we'd danced to. He drove with one hand, the other arm around me, and I wondered that he managed to find his way back to Skeld House. But he did, and put the car into the garage. We walked back to the house with our arms around each other. It was late enough to be dark, the darkest it grew these July nights. Inevitably, we stopped and kissed.

His lips were warm and smelled of beer. Mine did, too, I suppose. It was the first time I'd been kissed on the mouth since Dan. Maybe it brought back too much too painfully, maybe that was why I could not respond. I knew I mustn't let myself remember, I knew it was time to forget—

Screams shattered the stillness, shrill, high, staccato, the same monotonous note of terror over and over again. And then abruptly, silence.

We seemed rooted for an endless moment, and then the sound of a thud on the crushed stone of the driveway galvanized us. There were running steps; Jim took off in pursuit. But almost immediately a motor roared and raced, receding in minutes into the distance. Jim returned, still running, shaking his head, digging into his pocket for his key.

"Got away," he said grimly. "Looked as if he drove a van."

He opened the front door and plunged up the stairs, taking them two at a time. I followed as fast as my long skirt would allow. I was thinking, she's dead, Irene's dead.

Now I remember it as a tableau, complete. My bedroom door was open, and Irene was crouched in my chair, her hands over her face. Eugene loomed over her, not touching her, in his pajamas, his hair matted as if he'd been asleep. Mrs. Wall stared from the doorway, her hair loose on her shoulders so that she seemed younger and softer, breathing hard as if she had just rushed down from the floor above.

I found my voice. "Irene, are you all right?"

"Lisette! Oh, Lisette!"

I knelt beside her and she clutched at me hard.

"He came for me! He wanted to kill me!"

Involuntarily I looked up to Eugene. He turned away.

Jim said, "What the hell happened?"

"I don't know," Eugene said. "Ask Irene. I came when I heard her scream, and found her here."

Irene's hands tightened on me spasmodically. "There was someone in your room, Lisette. I couldn't sleep, and I thought you might have come back and I could ask you about the dance. I knocked and opened your door." She shuddered. "He threw me down and ran to the window."

"Did you see him?" Jim said. "What did he look like?"

"He had a stocking over his face. There was only the light from the window. He moved quickly, like an ape, heavy and powerful." She shuddered again.

"Did you call the police?" Jim said.

Eugene said, "I thought it could wait till morning. It's almost that now. It would take more than an hour for them to get here, and he's well away by now, if there was anyone here."

Jim caught it at once, as I did. "*If* there was anyone?"

"I didn't see him. Irene has hallucinated before."

I said tightly, "But we heard him! And Jim saw him drive away in a van!"

"You might have heard one of the servants. Clarke, for instance. He often visits Gerda in her room."

"Does he generally leave by the window?" Jim said evenly.

"You have no reason to think he did. You heard him on the driveway, that was all. And you think you saw him drive away. Clarke might have gone off somewhere."

"In the middle of the night? Where would he go to?"

"I haven't any idea," Eugene said. "You might ask him."

I had no heart to argue. I said, "Shouldn't Irene be given something to quiet her?"

"Mrs. Wall?" He looked cornered and hard-pressed.

She went at once to the bathroom and brought back a glass of water. From her pocket she took out a bottle and extracted a white pill, which she offered Irene. Irene turned her head.

"Let me." She gave me the tablet and I loosened Irene's clenched fingers and put it in her palm. She swallowed it then, and I was able to draw her back into her room and help her into bed. Eugene had said she hallucinated. Could he and Mrs. Wall be drugging her? How did I know what was in the pill I'd made her take? But how could it have been a hallucination? Jim and I had heard him, Jim had seen him drive away. Could it have been Clarke?

Eugene and Jim followed us to Irene's room, talking. Eugene's voice was audible in the quiet room. "If anyone did break in, remember, he broke into Lisette's room."

Irene's eyes opened. She said tiredly, as if the pill were already having its effect, "He came in through Lisette's room because it was dark, and I always have a light burning in my dressing room."

"Maybe so," Eugene said, "but it seems a lot more probable that he came into Lisette's room because it was Lisette's room he was interested in."

For a moment I was arrested; the idea hadn't occurred to me.

Irene's laugh sounded choked and harsh. "You *are* clever, Eugene. You've decided to make use of Lisette's predicament, and turn it to suit yourself. How beautifully it will work out—"

"Why don't you try and sleep," he said to her.

"Are you afraid I'll say too much, and give your plan away? But you won't fool Lisette, you see. She isn't stupid, and I've told her everything—"

Her voice had risen. "Irene, please." I went to her, my mind still stunned at the possibility that someone had tracked me down to Skeld House, had broken into my room. Was there to be no hiding out for me, anywhere? "Irene, it is possible that it was the notes he was after—"

She turned her face away from me. "You promised me you wouldn't let him fool you. You're as bad as he is. Please go away and leave me alone."

There was nothing I could do, nothing except let the sedative take its effect. After a while I followed the others, closing the door quietly behind me.

The window in my room was still open, and the room was very cold. I hurried to close it. My hands brushed damp earth with bits of grass still sticking to it, smeared across the sill.

Almost without thinking I ran out into the hall and knocked on Eugene's door. He hadn't yet gone to bed, and he looked at me with lifted eyebrows.

"I want to show you something," I said.

He followed me back to my room, and I showed him the mud on the window.

"Do you still think it was Clarke? If he was with Gerda, would he climb to her room through my window?"

He didn't answer. He said only, "I'll call the police in the morning."

I knew somehow he hadn't needed any proof, he'd known all along about the intruder. Heavy and powerful. Irene's description fitted the man Eugene had spoken with that first night.

❧ 8

Eugene telephoned the police and stayed behind to wait for them, and so we were all together at the breakfast table when Jarvie showed in a stout young man from the Zetland County Constabulary. He sat down and had some coffee with us while Jim and I told what we knew. When the policeman questioned Eugene, he deferred to Irene.

"My wife will tell you what happened. It was all over when I found her, so I can't be of any help."

Irene went over her story, calmer now, but an astute listener could still detect the suppressed hysteria in her voice.

After he'd heard what she had to tell, he looked over the house, examining my room and the mud still on the sill. Opening the window, he discovered a ladder flung aside below, which we'd missed in the darkness. He spent some time going over the grounds and outbuildings, and then he came back into the house to use the telephone. Jim overheard him reporting to someone about what had happened and talking about a possible check of all passengers leaving Lerwick or Sunburgh.

He shook his head doubtfully as he left. "It isn't like the island, to have something like this. We're a small place, and law-abiding, and we know every family. But then, it is the summer, and we get trippers, all kinds, and it is hard to detect the criminal element."

We didn't hear any more about it after that, so we concluded that the police had come up with nothing. But the incident was hard to forget. I might have had doubts about Irene and the reality of her fears, and how much was actual and how much a product of her obsession, but that someone had broken into the house was a fact. Whether he had come because of me or because of Irene there was no way of knowing. It was easy to believe he had come for the notes, but she had cried out that night against Eugene, accusing him of using my position to hide her own danger, and who could say for sure that she was wrong? Even if her fears were imaginary, even paranoid, she had presented tangible enough evidence that her life was in jeopardy. I was convinced that she wasn't lying, convinced she believed what she said. It seemed impossible to me that she could simulate terror that affectingly, even if she was an actress. And besides, there was the physical evidence of her deterioration—she couldn't simulate that.

Would I recognize a murderer, or a potential murderer, if I saw one? I wasn't any closer to knowing Eugene than I had been the day we arrived. When we talked together, we were host and guest, impersonal, formally pleasant. I didn't dislike him, as one does some people, almost instinctively sometimes. In fact I found him attractive, but then I've always liked quiet men. Quiet men suggest an inner life that is profound as well as private, reasonable, and thoughtful. Dan had been like that. Jim, by comparison, was all on the surface, amusing, attractive, easy to understand. If he went deeper, I hadn't discovered it yet.

Irene and I established our old relationship. The spell of good weather continued, and often I was able to coax Irene to leave the house. Now and then, when Jim would go off for the day with Eugene, we found the opportunity to talk more intimately than we could otherwise. One especially pleasant day I asked Mrs. Wall for some sandwiches, and Irene and I walked for almost an hour until we reached a cove where the rocks were flat and smooth as cloth. We opened our lunch there.

We talked about love and marriage.

"I was always bored with what I was sure of, don't ask me why," she said. "Even when I was in school. I would think of some boy constantly, pray every night for him to ask me on a date, and then, when he did, something went out of it, and I just lost interest."

I thought of Dan, and wondered whether it had been that consuming because we knew it would end and we would be separated. Would it have been the same without the threat of death hanging over us? No, it had to be more than that, more than a challenge and a chase, or what reason was there to share your life with someone?

I said, "When I think of Dan and me, it's always in such an ordinary way, like going to the supermarket together, wheeling a cart, carrying bundles home. Like getting away for a weekend in the car. Like waking up together on a snowy morning and not having to go anywhere."

She half smiled.

"You're so terribly wholesome, Lisette."

"You mean dull."

She shook her head soberly. "I wish I could have been more like you. I would have been satisfied, and what happened between Eugene and me would never have happened."

"Why didn't you ever have babies, Irene? Didn't you want them? Didn't he?"

I shouldn't have asked; her mouth tightened, she attempted a shrug but didn't answer. I said hurriedly, "I can imagine you didn't have the time, it was the kind of life you led—"

She cut me short. "You may as well know it, you know all the rest. I had one aborted, while I was still at Smith."

I said faintly, "I didn't know—"

"No one knew. It was still illegal then. My friend found a doctor through a friend of his, a nasty little man, but I was in no mood to shop around. You know Daddy, he's so terribly naïve, he would have died with the disgrace. Well, the doctor managed to infect me—I had peritonitis. And then, later, a regular surgeon removed a lot of me. So . . . no babies."

I remembered the time she'd had peritonitis. My mother had gone to see her every day when she was in the hospital. "I thought it was from your appendix."

"Daddy thinks so, too, and so does Eugene. Don't tell

him. I have enough black marks against me. Not that it would make any difference now."

We pushed the wrappings and her half-eaten sandwich under some stones, stood up, and were about to start back when Irene seized my arm and pushed me into the shelter of the rocks.

"Look. There she is again."

Mrs. Wall was pedaling her bicycle, close enough so we could see the covered basket strapped behind her. She couldn't have seen us, because we were below her line of vision and concealed by the rocks.

Irene said, "She's looking for me."

"Why should she be?" I tried to speak reasonably.

"I don't know why. Because Eugene has told her to. Maybe he thinks he'll surprise me with a lover." Her laugh had a touch of hysteria in it. "Some fisherman. Or sheepherder."

"But she knows we're together."

"She may think you're as corrupt and loose a female as I am."

I finally made her laugh with me. But she went back to it. "Then why does she come out after me? Is it just to hound me, persecute me? Maybe he hopes he can drive me away."

"But you said he didn't want to divorce you, that it wasn't enough for him."

"But if he drove me away, drove me out of my mind? What would happen to me? I'd be penniless, stuck in some institution, in one of those horrible gray sacks they wear, staring at nothing. That might please him. He knows how much I love beautiful things. He knows how much that would make me suffer."

She did seem to be haunted by her wealth and her fear of being deprived of it. I wondered at it, sick at heart. But Irene had always loved luxury. She used to coax Uncle Willy when she was still a girl to buy her the most expensive dresses, a fur coat, ski-holidays in midwinter at places like Gstaad and St. Moritz. He used to tell my mother that it was a good thing he didn't have a wife to support, that Irene managed to keep him broke. Eugene would be very much aware of the extravagance of her desires; he had known how to please her with that shower of jewels and clothes. But if he wanted to deprive her of them out of a need to hurt her, he had only to divorce her, he didn't have to persecute her or drive her mad. In any divorce suit he could cut her off with a minimum of settlement, which would be punishment enough for her.

Or would it? Did he need a deeper and more satisfying method? Her surmises seemed wild to me, but could there be some nugget of truth behind them? Could there be another personality behind that perfect control he showed, a person whom only Irene was in a position to know?

"She's coming back," Irene said. "She can't find us and she's going home."

Her basket was empty. "Or maybe," I said, "she finished her errand."

We stared at the small figure pedaling purposefully and quickly. Irene said, "I'm going to ask her, point-blank."

"What good would that do? She certainly won't tell you if she's been up to something."

"She will at least know that we've seen her."

"Irene—"

But she had already started up the slope in that spurt of feverish energy that always amazed me, and I could hardly keep up with her. Mrs. Wall didn't see us until we had practically put ourselves upon her path, for her head had been down, her face deep in thought. When she did see us, she braked suddenly and almost lost her balance, and her usual impassivity was momentarily lost.

"Where have you been, Mrs. Wall?" Irene said, almost insolently

The very insolence of her question seemed to restore Mrs. Wall's composure. "I've been out on my own time, Madam."

"I didn't say you weren't. I only asked where you had been."

"Where I go on my own time is my own business," Mrs. Wall said. "However, if you must know, I only went for a ride, to enjoy the fine weather."

She was so clearly the stronger of the two, and so much more in control of herself, that Irene felt it, and her voice reflected her helplessness. "Why are you always following me?"

"I wasn't following you, Mrs. Farrar. I had no idea where you were, except that you had gone walking with Miss Knowles."

"Irene." I had to get her out of this hopeless position. "We should be starting home ourselves."

Mrs. Wall's face was almost pitying. "Miss Knowles is right. You're a long way from home, and you shouldn't get overtired. If Clarke or Mr. Baird is home, I will ask either of them to come and fetch you home in the car."

She mounted her bicycle again and pedaled off.

Irene stared after her, her mouth pinched. "She won't get away with it. I'm going to find out what she was up to."

"You can't, Irene."

"I can follow her tire tracks."

She was right; we were able to make them out quite plainly on the spongy earth.

"Maybe she was telling the truth, Irene."

"There must be something," she said stubbornly. "I'm going to find it out, and when I do, she'll be sent packing."

The ground had given way to rocks again, a profusion of them, tumbling down to the water as far as we could see.

"If there's anything here, or anyone, we'll never find it. It would take days to search. Let's go back, Irene. We'll bring a car, and Jim will come with us."

But she had spotted something, tire marks not from a bicycle but from a car. They led downward, between the rocks, in a space that did not seem wide enough to admit a car. But it was there, the car, or rather a covered van.

A van. Jim had thought the intruder had made off in a van.

It was Irene who drew back first. She whispered, "Suppose he's in there."

"Wait here," I said. I crept around the rocks until I could find a place where I could see into the front windshield. She followed.

"No one's there," I whispered.

"He might be in the back, hiding."

There was no sound, just the short, mewing cries of the gulls.

I think I would always rather confront what I am afraid of than imagine it. Imagination has always seemed more terrifying than reality.

"I'm going to open the back of the van."

"You mustn't!"

"You wanted to see, Irene."

"I'm afraid."

But now it was I who had to see, if it would answer even one of our questions. We pressed close to the rocks, making no sound on the spongy soil, and reached the back of the van. We listened. No sound. I seized the handle and wrenched open the van door.

There was no one there. But the van held something, a rolled blanket, a plate with the remains of food on it, a cigar stub, a white napkin.

Irene had crept up beside me. "The monogram—'C' —'Cumberland'—the monogram on all our linen. The napkin comes from Skeld House."

The owner of the van was very real: he ate and slept here, he had some connection with Skeld House. He might even be hiding, watching us. Panic seized me suddenly, long overdue. I grasped Irene's arm, and we fled, almost running, turning back to look over our shoulders to see if we were being followed.

"There!" said Irene's stifled voice. "There! I see someone!"

Her fear infected me: it did seem as if I saw a shape, darker than the shadows of the rock. It might have been only a shadow. I pulled her along, not answering, afraid her legs would give out, afraid of her labored breathing.

Ahead of us a Land Rover appeared, coming from the direction of Skeld House. It was Jim, scouting the moor, looking for us.

He helped Irene inside, and we told him about the van and the napkin, and as soon as we reached the house, he telephoned the Lerwick police himself.

They sent the same plump constable who had come before; his name, we learned, was Muir. Again Eugene had nothing to contribute, gesturing to Irene and me to answer all Muir's questions.

"How did you happen to come upon the van?"

"My housekeeper was going in that direction." Irene lifted her head, flicking her glance over Eugene. "We wondered why, and we followed her path."

"I'll have a word with your housekeeper, if I may."

Eugene broke in, anger under the surface, "Mrs. Wall takes a ride everyday when the weather is good. She has the time. She's entitled to go wherever she wants."

"And the napkin from the house that we found in the van?" Irene's voice was high and thin.

Muir looked from one to the other. "It won't do any harm to ask, if you don't mind, Mr. Farrar."

Eugene tightened his mouth and was silent.

Mrs. Wall came in, quiet and unperturbed.

"Did you have any particular destination when you rode off today on your bicycle?"

She shook her head.

"You didn't happen to see a van such as Mrs. Farrar and Miss Knowles describe?"

"I saw no car. And no person."

He looked at her; he was bound to be impressed by her unshaken manner.

"There was a napkin from Skeld House in the van, with the Cumberland monogram on it. Have you any idea how it got there?"

She shook her head.

"Mrs. Farrar and Miss Knowles both say you had a linen napkin over your basket, covering it."

She said, "I took some tea biscuits along, wrapped in a paper napkin. I like to eat them as I ride. When I finished, I let the paper napkin fly away. But I don't know anything about a linen napkin from this house."

He couldn't ruffle her. After a few more questions he closed his notebook.

"I'll have a ride over to look for the van," he said. "Someone will have to come with me, to give me an idea where it was."

Irene and I looked at each other. She shook her head silently.

"I'll go," I said.

Eugene said, "I'd like to have a look at it myself. Will it be all right if I come along?"

Muir nodded.

"Are you all leaving me here alone?" Irene cried. "That man may be outside, waiting for you to leave!" Her voice was shrill.

"I'll be here," Jim said. "And there's a gun in the house, isn't there, Eugene?"

Eugene's face darkened. He nodded curtly.

"Where do you keep it?"

"It's in the table near my bed. You'll be careful?"

"I'm an excellent shot," Jim said.

Eugene's face looked preoccupied, even irritated, as we left the house. He had seemed more than normally disturbed over Jim's disclosure that he had a gun.

I sat up front because I had to direct the car; Eugene was in the back. I knew only roughly where to go; there were few landmarks on this sweep of fields. The *broch* had to be on our right, and the stones where we had eaten our lunch and first glimpsed Mrs. Wall had to be near the sea and unusually flat and smooth.

I found the stones only because one of us had been careless in covering our sandwich wrappings.

"Mrs. Wall came from that direction. I *think.*"

The car had a beam, which Muir shone ahead of us as we drove. The days had grown noticeably shorter, and the light was poor. There had been a tumble of rocks stretching for a long distance, marking a landfall. I saw them ahead of us, and pointed.

"You mean someone actually drove a car in among those rocks?" Muir said, good-naturedly enough, but plainly not believing it possible. "He must have been verra anxious to remain unseen."

We crawled slowly along the rim of rock outcropping. In my anxiety, I offered to get out and walk so that I could search for the tire marks more easily, and Muir agreed and stopped the car.

Somehow I did manage to spot the tire tracks; but I did not expect to see the van, and it was gone. There had been enough time for someone to warn the driver of our coming, or he might have seen us prowling about that afternoon and elected to leave. The tire marks were there and deeply marked, as if he'd been there some time, and there were even the ashes of a fire, stamped out and mixed with dirt.

"The tires are common enough, they'll be on half the vans in Lerwick," Muir said. "But we'll have someone out to take an impression at once, before it rains. Now what would a man be doing out here? Fishing, maybe. Camping out. We get many campers in the fine weather, and if it was a stranger, he'd have no way of knowing he was trespassing on Cumberland land."

Eugene said, "He might be birdwatching."

"Might be," said Muir.

I looked at them to see if they were serious. They were. I cried hotly, "Do birdwatchers usually break into houses with stockings over their faces?"

"But we do not know as yet if it's the same man," Muir said.

I suppose we didn't. We drove back to Skeld House in half the time it had taken us to locate the van. Eugene did not get out of the car.

"I'd like to drive to Lerwick with you if I may," he said to Muir. "I'd like to speak to your chief constable."

Muir seemed surprised, but he said only, "Come along if you want, then, sir."

I went into the house, brooding over what was in Eugene's mind. He would try to make light of the whole incident, maybe. Irene had been the only one to confront the intruder, and Muir must have observed how near hysteria she was. And, too, as Muir said, there was no evidence yet to connect the intruder with the van we found, except for Jim's brief glimpse of it as it had been driven away. If the marks of its tires were still on the grounds of Skeld House, they would be obliterated by rain and the tires of the other cars. Eugene was in an immensely influential position and, holding the power to benefit the islands, he might have the political weight to turn things to suit himself. Besides, everyone knew by now that Mrs. Farrar was in a nervous state, fearful in the solitude of Skeld House, and prone to highly colored imaginings. . . .

When I came into the drawing room, Jim and Irene were there. Jim jumped up.

"Did you find the van?"

I shook my head. "You wouldn't expect it still to be there."

Irene made a despairing exclamation.

"But they do believe it *was* there," I said. "Muir saw the tire marks and the fires someone built."

"Did Eugene say anything?"

"Nothing."

"Where is he?" Irene demanded.

"He went back to Lerwick with Muir. Some formality." There was no point in disturbing her with my suspicions.

After she went up to bed, Jim and I stayed on. He said, "I've been wanting to talk to Clarke. Since Eugene's away, would you like to have a word with him? I know Eugene must have got to him long ago, but we might catch something in his manner."

I thought it a good idea. As we walked down toward

the garage, I said, "Would Eugene try to influence the police?"

"He doesn't have to use any influence," Jim said. "All he has to do is tell them he'd just as soon drop the whole business. After all, it was his house that was broken into. If he doesn't want it followed through—"

He shrugged.

We climbed the stairs to the apartment where Clarke lived. His door was open, and he was lying on his bed listening to the radio. He got up when he saw us.

"Sorry. I didn't hear you ring."

"We didn't," Jim said. "Just wanted to ask you a question."

Clarke pulled out a chair for me.

"Remember that night when someone climbed in through the window? You are able to look down from here onto the spot where the van was parked, the one I saw him drive off in—I wondered if you'd seen anything."

"Not a thing," Clarke said cheerfully. "The cop from Lerwick asked me the same thing. I wasn't in my room, as a matter of fact. I'd spent the evening with Gerda, and then we walked back to the house. I didn't feel like sleeping, so I thought, what the heck, I'd take the Land Rover and go into Lerwick, maybe have a beer. You probably saw me drive away."

Jim said, "I saw a van."

"It's pretty dark."

"You didn't hear Mrs. Farrar's screams either?"

"You can't hear much from the house, with those thick

walls. And the motor noise would have drowned her out."

But we'd heard her screams outside. True, it had been quiet then. And the ladder? And the mud on the sill? Clarke was glib and casual, and it was all too smooth not to have been rehearsed.

There was nothing to say but thanks and good-night. At the door Jim turned. "Did you get your beer?"

Clarke grinned. "Everything was shut tight as a drum."

We went back to the house. We really hadn't expected more.

"If he's lying," I said, "the only reason he'd have would be because Eugene told him to."

"The whole story was nonsense. If Eugene hadn't had to improvise something fast for reasons of his own, he'd have come up with something better. Remember how he said it was Clarke he'd been talking to that first night we came? That was a spur-of-the-moment thing, too. He hadn't expected to be overheard. He knows that Irene would recognize Clarke, even with a stocking over his face. He isn't powerfully built, or apelike, as Irene described him, even discounting for her imagination. But why should he want to deny there was someone? Even to the point of going into Lerwick to convince the police?"

He had the same questions as I did.

He said slowly, "If there was anyone I know who I'd have said was not a liar, it would have been Eugene." He thought for a while. "Something had to have happened, something crucial, to change him."

"Suppose something did happen."

"I don't know. Irene was wild tonight. She made me go up and get his revolver, as if she needed to see it in order to feel safe. She said she was in some great danger, she said she was afraid of Eugene. She sounded so wild I began to be afraid for her sanity. She's far worse than I thought when I came here. Maybe she knows something we don't. Maybe she's losing touch with reality." He hesitated. "Of course there's the remote possibility that she's right and that she is in danger from him."

"Do *you* think she's in danger from him?"

"If you'd asked me that before this summer, I'd have said impossible. Now I'm not so sure. How about you?"

"I still don't see why he wouldn't settle for a divorce. How could he hurt her more than that?"

He hesitated. "You knew there was a man in Teheran who was her lover?" He saw on my face that I knew. "I figured you did. Irene told me about him, so she certainly told you. She blurted it out tonight when she was talking in that crazy way. I'd heard rumors before, but I couldn't believe them. They were so much in love, supposedly. But Irene can act without thinking, without thought of consequence."

"Would that man be enough to make Eugene want to kill her?"

"It isn't in his character. Or at least, it wasn't. But it might have been traumatic enough, crucial enough, to change him. He certainly went overboard when he met her. He might have gone just as completely overboard in the opposite way."

We were silent.

He said, "But then, why doesn't she divorce him? She could still get enough out of him to make it worthwhile, rather than stay on and put her life on the line. I think she's no longer capable of thinking the matter through lucidly. Why don't you urge her to leave him, Lisette?"

"We've talked about it. But she's still very much in love with him."

He whistled flatly, through his teeth. "I'm sorry for her, if that's the case. It's clear that he doesn't give a damn for her anymore. You'd think there'd be something left, if only pity, but if there is, I haven't detected it. I wonder why he wanted to bring her here."

"He said it's because she needs peace and quiet."

"He could have found peace and quiet for her without condemning her to solitary confinement. There's no reason for him to be here from a business point of view. He's always been interested in new developments, but he could easily fly down for a few days periodically and then leave."

He paused, and said ruefully, "They've certainly spoiled what might have been a very pleasant holiday. It isn't fair."

I agreed it wasn't fair. We tried to talk of other things, but it was impossible to detach ourselves from the events here, and we gave up finally and went back to the house.

I couldn't sleep. I didn't even try. I sat in the dark, leaning against the deep window reveal, and stared out over the moor. That was how I saw the police car return and let Eugene out. He didn't come into the house; he stood looking out as I did, his hands deep in his pockets, and then he walked slowly down to the wall that bordered the road.

I don't know why I did what I did. It hadn't been in my mind before. Thoughts that had come to me before crystallized. I didn't know him at all, only what Irene had told me of him. If I were to talk to him, perhaps I would have a better idea of the kind of man he was. Even if he lied I would know something, one way or the other. Maybe it was just because he seemed so lonely at that moment, and a lonely person is always approachable.

I couldn't allow myself to stop and reconsider or I would have lost my nerve. Quickly I let myself out of my room and ran downstairs, pausing only to put on my raincoat, which was hanging in the entry. He hadn't heard me coming across the soft turf, and looked up suddenly, startled.

I said the first words that came to my mind. "I wanted to ask you if . . . if they discovered anything."

"They've hardly had time." He added dryly, "Too much excitement for you? Couldn't you sleep?"

"No, I couldn't. But it wasn't excitement. I'm very worried about Irene."

"I'm sure you are."

"You must be, too. You're her husband. You can't just sit by and let her go on this way, let her . . . go to pieces."

He seemed to hesitate, and then he said, "It might be better if we talked somewhere else. If Irene were awake and were to see us, she would assume we were plotting against her."

Taking me by the arm, he led me back behind the gardener's shed, where we were hidden from the house. It was here that he must have been talking to the bald man. Was it because he wanted to be sure he would be unobserved from the house then too?

He began as if he had been formulating an answer:

"What makes you think anything can be done for her, any more than we have done already? She refused to work with psychiatrists. She has no medical problem. Remember," and his voice grew dry again, "if I seem less concerned than I should, I've heard her fantasize before, and I'm no longer shocked."

"I'm not thinking of her . . . stories. I'm aware that it may be fantasy."

"You're ready to concede that?" he said with dry amusement. "That she's not in any danger? That no one is trying to kill her?"

His amusement was at my expense, but I wasn't going to let it stop me. "I've never understood what is wrong with Irene. I don't know how much to believe of what she says. I only know that something has happened to make her ill. If I could know what it was, I might be able to help her." I hesitated, waiting for him to say something mocking, but he was silent. "I do want to help her, if I can. I can't bear to see her this way."

He studied me.

I swallowed. "I don't want to pry, honestly—"

"No, I didn't think you did," he said. "And I'm sure you want to help." And then, while I was still recovering from this unexpectedly conciliatory statement, he said, "What is it you want to know, exactly?"

It seemed wrong to attack him when he had offered that expression of confidence in me. I chose each word I said with care, so that my doubts would not sound belligerent and lose me the advantage I had: "You kept insisting that no one could have been in my room that night and knocked Irene down. And then you pretended it was Clarke, just as you pretended it was Clarke you were talking to that night when . . . when I don't think it was Clarke."

He heard me out, but I could almost feel him stiffening against me. When I had finished, he said, "It's my belief it was Clarke. He may have knocked her down by accident, or she may have tripped over her gown; she isn't always too sure of her footing. Clarke might very well have decided to leave by the window when he heard you come home if he'd been visiting Gerda in her room and didn't want to embarrass her. It's a guess, but it's the best I can do."

He was lying woodenly, badly, as if he were having trouble summoning up the necessary conviction. I was so sure he was lying that I went on, trying to cover the tremor in my voice.

"I'm sure you have a good reason for keeping the truth from me, and I know I don't have any right to speak to you like this. I wouldn't, except for Irene. Because if you're hiding something, covering something up, protecting someone, then . . . then Irene may be right, right in doubting you, and she may be right in believing she's in danger."

He lifted his shoulders and let them fall.

"You don't even deny it," I said.

"Would you believe me if I did?"

I said slowly, "I guess it doesn't matter if I believe you or not. It would help Irene if you could make her believe she isn't in any danger. You don't have to tell the truth to me. But do tell it to her."

"Irene has even less reason to believe me than you do.

What makes you think my reassurances would even get to her?"

"She *wants* to believe you. She loves you."

For an instant the silence hung between us. And then it was broken by his laughter. Speechless, I turned away, but he caught me by the arm and held me.

"You made a statement. At least let me answer you. If Irene told you she loves me, it isn't true. If you believe her, there's no way I can convince you otherwise. But I must say it: if she continues to live with me, it has nothing to do with love. What is more, Irene never loved me."

"Because of that single episode in Teheran? She told me about it, she told me how little it meant! She knows it was wrong, but she just wants you to forgive her and to forget what happened, and for things to be the way they were between you. I think that would make her well. I think she's sick out of guilt and misery."

He said, "You don't know a damned thing about it."

This time there was no doubt about his anger. I said, "No, I suppose I don't, and you don't intend for me to know."

I walked back toward the house, but he caught up with me before I reached the door.

"There's something else you should know, and it has nothing to do with Irene. You seem to take it very lightly, but you're the one in danger."

"From whom?" I said tightly. "Clarke? The bird-watcher?"

"You know from whom you're in danger. You're sensible enough to realize you may have been followed here."

"Thank you for warning me."

I started to pass him.

"Lisette."

Strange how his calling me by name was as if he had touched me.

"I'm sorry I laughed. But you don't know how absurd you sounded. You know nothing about us, and it's true that I prefer it that way. I never wanted you here to begin with, because I knew what it would lead to, but Irene asked you without consulting me, and then it was too late. I'm sorry if if I hurt your feelings. I apologize. You're a nice girl, not the kind of person I expected you to be, and I don't want to see you hurt."

His words continued to ring in my ears as I went up the dark stairway. Irene had told me that if he felt I didn't trust him, he would try to bring me around; she had told me how persuasive his charm could be. He was stubborn, he was impossible to reach, and he was lying; yet I was strangely shaken that night, as if he had marked me.

9

*I*f, as Eugene had suggested, the intruder, the man in the van, was after me, why didn't he approach me again? Why was he satisfied with an abortive attempt to search my room? Unless the notes had been found. But then I would have been told. Or, someone may have stolen them from my desk in the confusion of that day and already sold them, and so called off the man in the van.

More and more, as the days went on, I began to believe that. And more and more, as I thought of Eugene's evasiveness, I could see some truth in what Irene had said, that he might be laying stress on my danger in order to make light of hers.

Nevertheless I did not go out of the house on my own. A week passed, and with it came a growing sense of security.

Then a week of continuous downpour followed. We exhausted Scrabble, backgammon, and cards. Jim deserted us and went down to the works with Eugene, and one day, while Irene napped, I pulled on a slicker and rain hat and trudged down to the road. I had to breathe in some fresh air even if it was wet.

The ground had become boglike, and I stuck to the road that went to Skeld House. Ahead was a small, ruined chapel built by the original owner; there was no roof, and only a semblance of its pointed arches and buttresses. I thought I would head for it as a destination. Just then the rain increased into a solid sheet of water, and I bent my head and ran for the chapel and what shelter it could afford. That was the reason that I did not see the car, only heard its motor start.

I stopped and looked up. The car must have been parked behind the wall of the chapel, or I would have seen it on the road. The road from Lerwick circles and winds on flat moor, and Skeld House is above it all, on its knob of land. A car from Lerwick would be seen for a mile or two. Of course, I could have been mistaken; the visibility was poor in the rain. But I was sure I'd heard the sound of a motor starting up.

One of the servants driving back with supplies? Eugene? No, it wasn't any of our cars. This was a small English sedan, and we had only Eugene's large car and the Land Rovers. It was with that realization that I first felt alarm. I turned, and started back down the road to the house. It would have been quicker to have cut across the field, but I couldn't have made it today in that mire.

The car picked up speed, following me. It might just be a visitor to Skeld House, of course, but I was sufficiently alarmed to take no chances. I walked as fast as I could, still ashamed to show my fear and run, but as the car gained on me, I ran. The gate to Skeld House was only a hundred yards ahead when the car caught up to me.

"Is that Skeld House?"

The window had been rolled down, and a woman leaned out.

"Yes." I didn't stop walking at the same fast clip even as I answered. But the car kept up with me. I could see only that the woman wore dark glasses, and a rain bonnet that covered her fair hair.

"You sound American," she said. "So am I."

I knew I was ungracious, but I didn't dare take a chance. I continued to rush toward the gate without replying.

"I'm looking for Lisette Knowles."

"Who are you?"

"She doesn't know me," the woman said. "Actually I was told to ring her up when I reached the Shetlands by a mutual friend of ours, but the number is apparently unlisted, and they won't give it out, so I thought I'd just take a drive up and say hello."

"Who is the mutual friend?" I had to ask. I had to confirm in my own mind whether she was lying or not, or else that fearful starting at shadows that I had promised myself to stop would go on and on.

"Edna Wilson," she said easily. "We were at school together, though that was ages ago."

Edna Wilson, Beale's secretary, would not have given my address to anyone, even a close friend. Edna knew as much as Beale about my situation, and she was trusted by Beale because she was so closemouthed.

"I'm sorry, I can't help you," I said, and went in through the gate, latching it behind me.

She called out, "You are Lisette, aren't you? You're just as she described you."

I didn't turn around.

"Can't we talk for a minute? So I can tell Edna that I've seen you and how you are and what you've been doing?"

I ran toward the house and let myself in, shutting the door behind me. From the windows I watched the little car back and turn and go back toward Lerwick. If the woman was a friend of Edna's, then I had been rude and must even have seemed a little mad, but I was sure Edna would understand. And if she were not a friend of Edna's, then I *had* been followed, and the man who broke into the house might have been a confederate of this woman's. And Eugene was right.

Curiously, in view of our unsatisfactory meeting that night, and his lies and evasions, there was a subtle change in our relationship. In spite of the hostility of that meeting, barriers between us were not as firm. Maybe it was only that we each had revealed a little more of ourselves, but he no longer seemed to look at me with that cold curiosity, as if he were wondering if I had actually been capable of stealing Beale's notes, while I found myself more and more uncertain if he was in fact capable of persecuting Irene as irrationally as she had said. I distrusted my reaction: I wondered how much Eugene as a man had to do with it.

These thoughts would have been disturbing enough if I hadn't already had the fright of that encounter on the road, with all it signified. More, I had kept it to myself, I don't know why, waiting for the right time to tell them. And then Judy's letter came.

Clarke delivered it with the mail from Lerwick. I was surprised: my friend Judy is not a letter writer, as she freely admits. A scrawled postcard or an hour-long phone call are more in her style. The envelope from home stirred up memories of that last day in the office, but pleasurable emotions as well, because Judy had been my friend since high school and the only one to know where I was staying except my mother and Beale and the FBI. I took the letter to my room to read.

It was typed on office stationery, but then, Judy would choose to write on office time and on the typewriter.

She began:

I'm writing this in the office since it's business, not personal, but there'll be time to catch up on personal matters sooner than you can guess.

Something terribly urgent has come up, and I'm flying to Lerwick July 29th to meet you. I can't tell you any more now, but it's serious enough for Larris Foundry to pay my expenses to Scotland and give me three days off for it. I suppose you can guess what it is in reference to.

They've reserved Room 18 for me at the Royal Hotel. I'll be there by eleven o'clock and I'll have to catch the plane back that afternoon, so please come as promptly as you can. Just go right up to my room. Don't say anything to anybody at the desk. And don't say anything to anybody about where you'll be, even to your cousin. It's very important that we meet without anybody knowing. You'll find out why when I see you. I'm sorry that this has to be so hush-hush, but that's the way Beale wants it, and he says you'll understand.

There was a postscript:

Beale has just read what I've written. He says you should burn this after you've read it. J.

I reread the letter, looking for some inference I had missed. There was none. Cut-and-dried, it was the kind of letter Beale would have asked her to write, not the way she herself would have written at all.

Room 18. Royal Hotel. July 29th. That was all I had to remember. I tore the letter up into small pieces and put them in the fireplace and set a match to them. Of course, it had to do with the notes, but how? Could they have been found? Then why did she have to talk to me? Unless I had to study them, maybe to see if they were the originals, not a copy. But couldn't Beale tell that? Maybe not. I had observed them more minutely in order to transcribe them. And if they were still lost, had something happened they had to tell me about, so secret that they did not dare trust a telephone call?

I could come up with no answers. July 29th was Monday. I had two more days to wait, to find out. In a way, it gave me something else to concern myself with, to take my mind off the situation at Skeld House and my own feelings.

I told no one about my intentions to drive into Lerwick on Monday morning. Eugene had left early, as usual. Irene and Jim and I lingered over our breakfast coffee, and I waited until I found an opening to say casually, "Could I borrow one of the Rovers, Irene? I thought I'd go into town and shop for some gifts. That Fair Isle knitting—"

I knew it sounded strange that I didn't ask Irene to join me, even though she never went to Lerwick. Or Jim: he had mentioned that night of the Coast Guard Ball that he'd like to join me when I chose a day to go there. I had to disregard them both today, no matter what.

Irene said at once, "Of course. You don't have to ask," but Jim did look at me oddly.

So oddly that I thought it necessary to speak to him before I left.

"I just felt I had to get away. And it's best that one of us stay with Irene. She hates to be left alone."

He accepted my explanation at once.

"Place getting you down?" he said sympathetically. "I thought you were a bit quiet these last few days."

He brought the car around to the house for me. "Sure you can handle the gears?"

I could, or at least I would be able to if I went slowly and practiced shifting. I'd once dated a boy with a sports car, and he'd taught me how to drive it. I was sure I would remember.

"I'll be back by late afternoon." I was leaving myself enough time to shop after I left Judy, so that there'd be no question as to why I'd gone to Lerwick.

My excitement began to mount as I drove, not only because of what she had to tell me, but because of seeing her again. I had always talked intimately with Judy, and she with me: it would be good for me to tell her about Skeld House and Irene and Eugene. It might clarify my own thinking to talk about them and to hear her reaction; I knew whatever I told her would be held in strict confidence. The day was bright; sunlight glinted off the windshield, and on the glimpses of the sea. Judy would wonder about some of the things I'd written in my letters to her; the Shetlands could present two entirely different faces, depending on the weather.

I parked the Land Rover at the pier, where it would be less likely to be observed. It was possible that people might recognize the shield of the Cumberlands on the door, or at least notice it. It was still early, about a quarter of eleven, and I looked into the windows of one of the knit shops to see what I could buy on my way home. But I was impatient, my heart beginning to thump, and so I walked up the hill to the Royal even though it was still a few minutes to eleven, and went in.

Fortunately, the lobby was crowded, and the man behind the desk was busy at the telephone. I slipped up the wooden stairway to the rear without anyone stopping me, and walked down the dim corridor looking for Room 18.

The door was open, and on the luggage rack I could see a BOAC flight bag.

"Judy?" I tapped on the open door. No one answered, and I went in. "Judy?" Maybe she was in the bathroom; the door was open and I went toward it. "Judy?"

The hall door closed. I whirled around. Judy is tall, and is always changing her wigs from blond to redhead, so I did think it was Judy at first, from the back.

"You *are* being very hush-hush," I began, when she turned around, but it wasn't Judy. Even without the sunglasses and the rain bonnet I knew at once it was the blond-wigged woman who had come to Skeld House.

"Won't you sit down, Miss Knowles."

My legs felt weak. I sat down.

She sat opposite me. She was in her forties, big-boned and handsome, undistinguished, with a hard mouth and a fixed jaw. Her hair, as I'd suspected, was Dynel.

"I'm sorry I had to bring you here this way, but you did refuse to wait and hear what I had to say to you."

I found my voice. "Who are you?" I said, as I had the other time.

She still wouldn't say. "It doesn't matter. It wouldn't be my name, anyway. I'm sure you know why it was important to have this meeting."

"I have no idea."

She smiled a little. "But you came."

"I came only because Judy asked me to."

"And you told nobody?"

I hesitated, wondering if I should lie, wondering which answer would be the safer. But she read my hesitation correctly, and went on in the same brisk manner.

"You told nobody because Judy asked you not to. Good."

"You wrote the letter?"

"It was written by the people I represent."

"Who are they?"

"That doesn't matter to you. It's better for everyone concerned if they remain anonymous. I am empowered to act for them."

"Are you American?" I marveled at my composure. I

suppose, without my realizing it, I had been living and reliving this very situation in some form or other since the FBI's visit; it seemed familiar to me. What I hadn't been prepared for was this woman: I had imagined men, Slavic, bullet-headed, or urbane Chinese. Her strong, hard features under a Judy-like wig and wearing a Judy-like pants suit were what had shocked me, what still shocked me as I looked at her. "You speak like an American." If there was anything strange about her speech, it was its perfection; her accent was pure American.

"Let us just say that I have lived in America for a great many years. Now to business. The interests I represent are prepared to pay a large sum of money for Geoffrey Beale's notes. Fifty thousand dollars."

My voice was calm. "I don't have the notes."

"I don't want to waste time. Seventy-five thousand."

"I told you, I don't have them. There's no use your asking me."

"I can offer you up to one hundred thousand," she said, without inflection. "That is my limit."

"Even if I had them, I wouldn't sell them to you."

I stood up, and she did too.

"Stay where you are, please."

I disregarded her and went to the door, my heart beating hard. She reached it before I did and faced me, and she held a short black revolver in her hand. I had imagined it often, this scene, but my coolness deserted me now, and I was overwhelmed by fear.

"And now will you sit down again?" she said. "I have used this before, and I assure you, I have no qualms about using it again if I have to. Try to make a sound and I shoot. The gun has a silencer. I can be gone from here long before they discover your body."

She gestured toward the chair I had left, and I returned to it numbly. My mind raced over the probabilities. She could kill me, hide my body—in the wardrobe? in the bathtub? change her wig and her dress and maybe even her passport—didn't they always come prepared with a second passport? and board the plane from Sunburgh long before the chambermaid came that evening to turn down the bed. Did the chambermaids in the Royal Hotel turn down the beds?

"Your handbag, please."

I pushed it toward her. The gun held unwaveringly in her right hand, she pulled everything from my bag with her left, examining each pocket, reading each shred of paper. With a razor blade that lay on the desk she slashed the lining and groped under it. Her face reflected her disappointment. She pushed everything roughly back and tossed the bag onto my lap.

"You're making it difficult for yourself as well as for me. If you give up the notes now, you can return to Skeld House at once, and unharmed. We are safe, and you are safe. No one will ever know that you have given them to us. But if you persist in being stubborn, we shall have to get them another way."

"You've already searched my room—"

"I?" she said. "Not I. Has someone else been there? Perhaps others know about them. But I was assured . . . our sources said there was no other leak but to us." She became suddenly agitated. "Has anyone else been after them? Have you received a better offer?"

"I did not take any notes. You're wasting your time."

"We know that you have them," she said. "You will not leave this room unless you have turned them over to us or told us how we may get them. Take off your dress." She gestured impatiently with the revolver.

"But why—"

"I will search you now. Hurry." She gestured with the revolver again.

I had no choice. I stood up and began to unbutton the cardigan I wore.

The sound of a key turning in the lock of the bedroom door was audible in the silence. We both turned our heads, startled, as a chambermaid stuck her head in.

"Sorry, Madam. I'll just put these towels in the bathroom if I may—"

As I try to remember that moment, I don't remember making a decision to act, to move. The chambermaid was apologetically darting into the bathroom. I saw that the gun had disappeared and that the eyes of my captor looked disconcerted. I ran.

I ran down the hall, down the steps. I looked up once and saw her reach the top of the landing. I didn't wait to see if the gun was in her hand; I ducked around and out of her sight. The desk clerk was looking at me with his mouth open. I was aware of heads turning as I ran. I didn't care about anyone, about my blouse half buttoned and my wild appearance. Gasping for breath, I saw a tea shop ahead, crowded with tourists. I slipped inside, and chokingly asked if there was a telephone.

There was, on the wall. I thought of the police. But I

didn't want the police to know, not yet. I called Skeld House.

Jarvie answered.

"May I speak to Mr. Baird? This is Lisette Knowles."

"Mr. Baird has gone walking with Mrs. Farrar. Will you leave a message?"

"When will he be back?"

"He didn't say. Mrs. Wall packed some sandwiches."

I thought frantically. "Is Clarke there?"

"Clarke drove Mr. Farrar to the works."

That was the first time I thought of Eugene. "Do you happen to have the telephone of the works?"

"Yes, Madam, I have it right here."

He gave it to me, and I called the number, watching fearfully each time someone appeared at the shop door.

A man answered.

"Is Mr. Farrar there?"

"I'll have a look. Who's calling?"

"Lisette Knowles."

I hung onto the phone as if it were a lifeline. Suppose he weren't there? I dared not go back to my car; she or a confederate might be watching it, and even if I could get safely into it and away, I had no way of knowing that they might not be lying in wait for me along the road. I couldn't bring the police in: I wanted to keep the notes as secret as I could from the authorities here. There was nothing to do but stay hidden until someone rescued me, but how long could I hide? When the lunch-hour jam ended, I would be exposed.

"Yes?"

Eugene. I could hardly speak in my relief. "Would you please come to Lerwick and get me? Please?"

He must have surmised something was wrong from my voice, even if my words hadn't been so odd. He didn't stop to question me, but said at once, "Where are you?"

I craned to see the name on the window. "MacGowan's Teas. Down the street from the Royal Hotel. Please hurry!"

"It will take me half an hour." He hung up abruptly.

It was an endless half hour. I had tea seated at a table well in the back, and later, as the crowd thinned out, I darted into the ladies' room. I took a long time, straightening my clothes, arranging my papers in my slashed handbag, splashing my white face with cold water. When I looked out after a while, Eugene was opening the shop door.

I ran to him and clutched him, almost crying out in my relief. He didn't speak, only took me out quickly to the car parked outside and put me in, and came around to his side at once and started the motor. He still asked no questions, only, "Shall I drive you back to Skeld House?"

I nodded, and as the car moved forward toward the Royal Hotel, which we would have to pass, I cowered down in my seat, afraid for even my head to show through the glass.

Outside the Royal there seemed to be a commotion, and people were milling about the entrance and in the street. A police car was parked near the door, and an ambulance was backed onto the curb.

We slowed to a crawl to pass, and even as we did, two hospital attendants came out carrying a stretcher with someone bundled in a blanket lying on it. I sat up to look. A strand of blond Dynel hair escaped from the blanket around the white face. . . .

I must have made a sound, because Eugene turned to look at me. He braked the car, rolled down his window, and leaned out.

"What's the trouble?"

A man walked over to the car, touched his cap. "Some woman was roughed up in her room. They say she is an American, a tourist. They say, too, that the room was fairly torn apart, so it must have been robbery, but the lady is still unconscious, and there's no telling if anything was taken."

"Was she hurt seriously?"

"They dinna say so. Knocked unconscious is what I heard."

The car started forward again, moving slowly until we had cleared the knots of onlookers, and then gathering speed as we left the town behind. He waited until then to say, "Do you know something about what happened? Is that why you're frightened?"

There was nothing to do but tell him everything. I think I wanted to, I had to. He listened without comment. I said, "I don't know what happened after I ran out of her room. But I'm sure it had something to do with me and the notes." I turned my head away and indulged in a bout of nervous crying.

He still said nothing, until I blew my nose and wiped my face and sat up. Then, "Could the chambermaid have been involved, somehow?"

"I don't know. But I don't think so. I mean, she *looked*

like a chambermaid. And acted like one. And her speech was from around here, I think."

"Did you hear her knock?"

"No, but she might have. We were both so intent on each other that we might not have heard her."

"So she might have knocked, and not hearing a reply, just barged right on in. And saved your skin. It could have happened that way, one of those unforeseen accidents." He looked down at me. "Feeling better?"

"Yes. My head hurts a little."

"You were lucky this time. I did warn you."

"But the letter was from Judy—" I faltered. "Or, I thought so."

"Right, and the next time, the excuse to get you might seem equally plausible."

"I don't understand who could have attacked her. Or *why?*"

"It might be someone who followed you, someone who knew you were going to meet a person in the Royal Hotel. Someone who thought the notes had changed hands, that you had sold them, or had been made to give them up."

"But then they must have seen me running for my life! Would I have run away like that if I had handed over the notes?"

"What makes you think you would be out of danger if you sold the notes?" he said dryly. "It would be to their best interests to dispose of you."

That silenced me for a while. I don't know why I asked him then, but I did: "Do you think I have the notes?"

He took his time replying. "I did think so, at the time

when Irene told me about them. She'd heard from your mother, and your mother said you were so distraught that she was afraid for you. A person in that frame of mind might do anything."

"Even if I were that distraught, I doubt I could be a traitor."

"No, I don't think you could be."

His glance was long and level. I felt the blood rush into my face.

"Don't forget, I didn't know you," he said. "All I knew was that you were Irene's cousin, and remember, I haven't much reason to believe in her integrity or incorruptibility."

Moved as I was by gratitude for his trust in me, I still had to defend Irene. "Are you being unprejudiced toward her? Maybe she is thoughtless, and even selfish, but she couldn't do anything really bad. I know her. She's sick now, and muddled, but even so—"

"She's an amoral woman," he said. "I don't mean that in any priggish sense, but in a deeper way. She will do whatever gives her pleasure or satisfies her at the moment, and she won't stop to consider the consequences to anybody, even to herself or the larger aspects. She's self-indulgent. Even her bringing you here was an act of self-indulgence. I still don't know why she asked you, but she had a reason."

I hid my feeling of dismay at his words, even as I wondered if there was any truth in them, or if he felt he had to destroy her image to me. "She had to have someone to talk to. And she needed someone to—" I stopped, and reddened.

"To protect her against me. So she asked you and Jim to come."

"In her state of mind, does it seem strange?"

"You asked me a direct question before. Now I'll ask you one. Do you think Irene has any reason to be afraid of me?"

How could I answer, after his expression of confidence in me? I faltered. "I don't understand how . . . how you can be so cold to her, so indifferent to her condition. You do act . . . as if you hated her. I know she isn't as beautiful as she used to be—"

He broke in brusquely. "I don't hate her. And I still find Irene a beautiful woman." He hesitated, and when he spoke it was with difficulty. "There was a time, once, when I believed that loving Irene and marrying her was the greatest piece of luck that could have happened to a man."

I was shaken by his utter conviction.

"When I was young I was offered the chance to run my father's company. I may have been too young, but I wanted to do it, wanted to meet the challenge. I had to give it all my energy, all my attention. And then I met Irene."

He frowned.

"I can't explain it, but it was as if she showed me a world I'd forgotten even existed. I lost my head. That's the only way I can put it. Maybe I was ready for her, maybe the business was under control, but it was a complete reversal for me, and suddenly nothing mattered but her. I couldn't see her for the woman she was. Even when I found out, I refused to believe it, I fought it. I wanted to believe she was the woman I thought I married, and it took some shattering revelations before I finally accepted the truth."

He spoke with such passion that I had no argument. I said troubledly, "But Irene never pretended to be perfect. You insisted that she was, and when she wasn't after all, you blamed her. I know she was wrong, but was she so wrong that you have to keep punishing her, and yourself?"

For a moment I thought he would laugh at me again.

I said in a low voice, "If I sound naïve and foolish to you, it's only because I don't understand. Don't patronize me because I don't know—"

"You don't know," he repeated, and suddenly he seemed tired. "It has to be that way. Between Irene and me."

We finished the drive to Skeld House in silence. But Eugene had changed, to me. In the back of my mind reason told me he had explained nothing, but rather he himself had admitted to such a fierce love for her that he might be driven to an act of destructive violence, such as Irene feared; he had given credibility to her story. And yet I would always see him as the man who had walked in the door of MacGowan's Tea Shop, I would see him as someone who thought I was a nice girl who would never betray her country, as someone to whom my life was a matter of concern. When Skeld House and the unhappiness and fear it contained loomed in front of us, I was almost sorry that the drive had come to an end.

We settled on an explanation of our coming home together. I'd had trouble with the gear shift and had been afraid to drive the car back. It was partly true, and Jarvie would confirm that I'd telephoned and asked first for Jim and then for Clarke before I'd asked for Eugene's number. The events of the day should remain secret: the servants might overhear, and it was best for me that nothing leak out about what happened at the Royal Hotel. If I'd brought no gifts back from Lerwick, the ostensible reason for going there, I had just seen nothing I wanted.

Eugene stopped me as we went in. "Let me warn you again. That woman may have confederates. If she knows where you are, so may others. Don't go anywhere alone. I'm going to tell Clarke to stay at Skeld House from now on."

This time I did not take his warning skeptically or defiantly. I agreed. I said soberly, "I never thanked you for coming to get me. I don't know what would have happened if you hadn't been there."

"I hope you would have had the good sense to get in touch with the police, and the devil with secrecy about the notes. Your life is what matters."

Matters? To you, too? I met his eyes.

He said, "I kept imagining all sorts of things as I drove to meet you. I was afraid I might be too late."

The moment lengthened.

"They must be wondering what we're talking about," I said faintly.

We went inside. We could hear Jim and Irene in the drawing room, but Eugene went past without stopping.

I lingered, telling them what a time I'd had with the car.

"I've got a bit of a headache," I said. "Maybe I'll skip dinner tonight."

I was having a delayed reaction to my experience at the Royal. There was more to it, more than I was prepared to acknowledge even to myself. I lay on my bed and watched the aquamarine sky deepen into dusk, thinking, thinking, to the accompaniment of my throbbing head.

❧ 10

I hadn't intended to tell Jim about what happened at the Royal Hotel, but he brought it up.

Again it was in the local newspapers that he read about it, an attack on an American tourist whose name was withheld because of her wish not to alarm her family. She had recovered and returned home, the paper said. I suppose my face must have revealed my relief that she was gone, because I thought Jim glanced at me with curiosity. It was only later when we found ourselves alone that he asked me about it point-blank.

"That was the day you were in Lerwick," he said. "Did you hear or see anything?"

I shook my head, unhappily.

"And that was the night you stayed in your room, with a headache, they said."

"Do you think I attacked her?" I said, trying to laugh.

"No. I just wondered if there was a connection."

After all, he knew everything else, even more than I had ever told Eugene or Irene, so I told him what happened. He listened thoughtfully, now and then giving a low flat whistle of amazement.

"I don't think I could have passed it off that coolly."

"I wasn't that cool, honestly. It just seemed so . . . so *expected*. I suppose I didn't really know what danger I was in."

"You seem like such an innocent to get involved in such heavy matters, like international intrigue. I never took it seriously, really seriously."

"Apparently some people do."

"I never realized there'd be so much money involved," he said. "Eugene's probably right. An interested party might be ready to pay a million for them."

"I wouldn't take a million for them. *If* I had them."

He smiled. "But then they don't know the kind of girl you are. They may think you're the usual soulless, conscienceless, politically immoral traitor." He sobered. "Look, don't tell any of this to Irene. She has her own problems without having to worry about you."

I agreed.

"Anyway," I said, still thinking about his words, "if I were bitter about my country and vindictive enough to betray it, I'd do it for nothing. Money wouldn't be the reason."

"Not even a million? You must be very rich."

"Hardly," I said. "Not that I've ever been deprived, and I've been independent of my mother ever since I started working. No, I think it's because I've never needed that kind of money. Maybe I'd have been different if I'd have been beautiful, like Irene. When you're beautiful, you need a beautiful setting, clothes and furs

and jewels, and the kind of life that goes with them. I just
. . . never wanted them."

He said, "I've been looking all my life for a girl like
you."

I retreated, hastily. "Not that I would turn down an
emerald if someone offered it to me. Or a trip around the
world. I just don't feel I couldn't live without them."

He slipped his arm around me. "There must be something you want. I refuse to believe you don't want anything, it simply isn't possible."

There was a time when I might have answered him
more easily. Dan and I had talked about the things that
were important to us, like the work you did, and how it
must be important to you and meaningful enough so that
you could spend your life doing it. And there were dreams
of a house with more rooms than we needed, and windows looking out on something beautiful, like water, like
hills. Dan . . . he himself seemed almost like a dream to
me, slipping away from me. I said, "If I want anything
now, it's to be loved. And to love someone."

"Have anyone in mind?"

His face loomed close, as attractive as a girl might
conjure up, but inexplicably I saw Eugene as he had
looked that day he came to rescue me from MacGowan's
Teas. Disconcerted, and momentarily speechless, I shook
my head.

"You might fib, to save my face."

"You don't need to have your face saved, and you know
it. Anyway, you never told me what *you* want, since it's
so impossible not to want something."

He grinned. "If I told you, it would only embarrass you,

so I had better keep it to myself. Let's just say I have a dream of fair women, and the leisure and money to enjoy them. And speaking of fair women, will I see you when we get back to New York?"

"I don't see why not. But are you coming back?"

He shrugged, and his expression darkened suddenly. "I'll be looking for a job, I guess. Eugene hasn't been exactly eager to make me an offer."

"Have you spoken to him?"

"He puts me off whenever I bring it up. I hate to say this about my distant cousin and host, but I think he enjoys the sense of his own power. He's been damned skillful about manipulating business deals, and maybe he's extending it now to personal relations. I suppose he's hardened with the years, he was at the top at too young an age, and now he thinks he's God and can dispense judgments."

Can he dispense judgment on Irene and condemn her to death for her sins? I shivered at my fanciful notion.

"What's worse, he seems to enjoy having me on the hook, making me beg for it. Sometimes I think Irene soured him on the world, and he has to make others pay for his own unhappiness. But why should I be surprised? If he can treat Irene as he does, why should he be any kinder to me?"

Jim wasn't overemotional; he was sane and down to earth. If he could think of Eugene in this way, I should be more ready to believe what Irene thought. Maybe I was just flattered by his interest in me, maybe I was being romantic and unwilling to face the truth, maybe I was more ready than I thought to succumb to his compelling semblance of sincerity, maybe. . . .

I went to bed and was overcome by depression. I got up, looked for a sleeping pill, and finding none, went across to Jim's room. He wasn't asleep: I could hear his transistor radio playing, and so I tapped on his door.

It was then that I heard the laughter from Irene's room, harsh and mirthless, more like weeping, broken and wild. I was afraid to go to her, afraid she wasn't alone.

Jim opened his door.

"What the devil's going on down there?"

"It's Irene."

He made a move as if to go to her, but I held his sleeve. "Should we interfere? Eugene may be with her."

"He hasn't been in her room in years."

Suddenly there was a dull thud, and a cry. Jim shook off my hand and ran to her room. I followed.

Her door flew open as we reached it, and Irene stumbled past us, holding her hand dazedly to her cheek. A thin trickle of blood ran between her fingers. She did not seem to see us, but clutching the banister, she made her way down the stairs while we watched, stupefied. She pulled open the front door and was outside before we knew what was in her mind.

Jim went after her. I paused, my eyes held by Eugene in dressing gown and pajamas, standing in the open door between his room and hers. And then I turned, and ran down the stairs.

Outside there was just enough gray starlight to make out her white-gowned figure racing toward the moor and the headland and the sea. She was barefoot, and incredibly swift, but Jim was catching up to her. I stopped and waited, watching them, heavy-hearted.

In that moment I had the sense of someone close to me. I don't know what made me so sure: a movement behind the shrubs? cigar smoke? The gardener's shed was nearby. The thought of someone hiding behind it made my blood run cold.

Jim had reached Irene and was returning with her, carrying her in his arms. Maybe that gave me courage: he was within call. I ran around to the front of the shed and pushed open the door. The evidence of a man's presence was even stronger: damp woolen clothing, boots, sweat. It could have been Nichols, true, but the gardener couldn't have been here for hours now, and strong winds brought their own smells of salt and grass and water, sweeping away everything else. He would have to have been here only moments ago. I reached in and felt for the switch and snapped it on. There were piles of sacks, and boards leaning against the wall, and shadows where a man might hide, but I did not think he was here anymore. He could have slipped out and lost himself among the shrubs while I was frozen into immobility.

I turned out the light and caught up with Jim and Irene. She was unconscious, her mud-stained feet dangling lifelessly, blood spotting her white gown. In the lighted hallway Eugene watched us come back, somberly.

"For God's sake, man," Jim said between his teeth, "for God's sake, how could you?"

Eugene didn't answer.

In her room, Jim put Irene down on her bed. The room

smelled sour. She must have vomited earlier, because her sheets were fouled. He threw open a window, and I covered her with the stained quilt. I didn't know where anything was; I ran upstairs to get Mrs. Wall.

She must have been awake before I knocked, because she was already putting up her hair. I almost felt that she had seen Irene's wild flight from her window and had begun to dress to come down.

We returned together to Irene's room, and she went to work efficiently, as if she had done this before, stripping the sheets from her bed, moving her body from side to side.

"She's asleep," she said briefly, because I was watching, still alarmed at her heavy, erratic breathing. "She'll be all right when she wakes up."

"How can you be sure?" I cried.

She looked up, and her glance went past me to Eugene, who had come in unnoticed. It seemed to me that their eyes conveyed some message to each other.

"She should have a doctor," I said. "I think you should call a doctor at once."

Eugene lifted his shoulders and let them fall in a gesture that was like resignation. "I'll telephone Granby. Clarke will have to go and bring him. He would never come out at this time of night."

He went past Jim without turning his head, and we could hear him telephoning from his room. Jim wandered outside, while I stayed behind with Irene. Mrs. Wall had finished changing Irene's gown and putting a fresh quilt over her. The room was cold, and she shut the windows again and drew the blinds. Something glinted on the floor; I went over and bent down to see. Tiny particles of thin glass—

"Something must have broken."

Mrs. Wall glanced where I pointed. "I'll take care of that," she said quickly, and with a napkin she held in her hand she sponged up the slivers of glass. The cold was penetrating, and I went to the fireplace and poked the gray wood into flame.

I was a fool. I had let my sympathies go out to Eugene, and he had made me believe him and doubt Irene.

Mrs. Wall was gathering up the soiled linen, her face unreadable. I thought, how she must hate Irene! Not because Irene disliked or distrusted her, but because Irene was everything she was not. Her pinched mouth and sallow skin, her gray-laced hair drawn uncompromisingly back, all a silent admission of failure to win any man's admiration, let alone Eugene's. If she had ever loved him, how heartbreaking it must have been for her when he brought Irene into his house. I found myself pitying her.

I said, "Will she be all right?"

"You needn't be concerned. She will, I'm sure."

"How did it happen? Is it a concussion? Could she have struck her head when she fell?" If Eugene had anything to do with it, I did not expect Mrs. Wall to say so, and my questions were as much to make some communication between us as anything else.

She said, as I expected, "You will have to ask Dr. Granby when he comes."

"It seems odd, that so many terrible things happen to her—"

She straightened up and met my glance evenly. Her

voice was harsh. "Mrs. Farrar is her own worst enemy. She had everything a woman could want to make her the happiest person on earth. Beauty, wealth, a fine man to love her. She treated them like dirt beneath her feet. Whatever happens to her, it is her own doing only."

She went out, and I tried to get more warmth out of the fading fire.

I was waiting near the window to watch for the doctor, and so I saw the headlights of the car from a distance, winding through the dark moor. The car let the doctor out at the door, and he entered the house, a short, bluff man who must have put his jacket and trousers over his pajamas, because the striped cotton ends stuck out. He motioned me from the room brusquely and asked for Mrs. Wall, as if he knew her, as if this had happened before.

I went downstairs, where Jim joined me, and we stood together hardly talking until Irene's door opened and Dr. Granby emerged and came down the stairs. Eugene appeared; he must have been waiting too.

"She's asleep," Granby said to the question on our faces. "I didna try to wake her, but she will be better in the morning." He put down his bag in order to button his coat high. Reproachfully, he said, "It wasna necessary to send for me at this ungodly hour."

I reddened. "It was my fault. But she was irrational."

Granby looked at me a long moment, and then at Eugene.

I plunged on, "Shouldn't you take some analyses? This has happened before—"

"Yes, and it will happen again unless more precautions

are taken to watch her. Someone must be with her every minute of the day, as I told you before." His voice was curt. "As for any further tests, they are not necessary. I've found the drugs she uses from time to time, and they are of the amphetamine type. You need only to roll up her sleeve if you need any further evidence." He picked up his bag. "Good night."

I watched the outer door close behind him, and then I sank down on the bottom step of the staircase.

Jim spoke, as shocked as I, "I can't believe it."

To my consternation, Eugene turned on him, his voice thin with anger. "Come off it, Jim! Are you trying to tell me you didn't know what was wrong with Irene? You knew back in Teheran!"

Jim's face paled. "I swear—"

"You knew the crowd she ran around with! What they did, the kind of people they were—That was no secret to you."

"I didn't know them! I wasn't in on their secrets! I didn't have the time or money to be part of any circle Irene played around with! What's more, I didn't have the inclination! I got my kicks the normal way!"

His furious denial died away. I stared at Eugene, still dumbfounded. He seemed almost less certain than he had been.

"Would you mind telling me where you get your ideas about me and my habits?" Jim cried.

"I've been told," Eugene said. "My sources could have been mistaken." He added, "If it isn't true, I'm sorry I said it, and I apologize."

"Are you sure you didn't cook up the idea yourself? Are

you sure you're not so damned twisted up inside that you're beginning to imagine things?"

"I told you that someone told me that, and if he was wrong, I'm sorry."

"Why the hell did you invite me to your house, if you believed that of me?"

"If I had known about it in time, I wouldn't have. Look, can we forget about it? This has been a tough evening for all of us."

"Maybe your source of information got other matters cockeyed too," Jim said. "Is that why I'm not being considered for a better job? Maybe you ought to question your spies a little more carefully!"

Eugene moved toward the stairs, his head bent. "This isn't the time to talk about your job."

"There hasn't been a time all summer!"

Eugene only shook his head and went on upstairs.

Jim stared after him, his white face working in futile anger. "I didn't know Irene in Teheran! I didn't know she was on drugs. I thought it was a bug, and maybe too much drinking—He had no damn right to talk to me like that —" He stopped. "Hell, I'm getting out of here. First thing in the morning."

In a panic I ran to him. "Don't go, Jim! I couldn't stay here without you! And I can't leave Irene now!"

"I don't want to have to face that bastard again."

"He did apologize. He said it was a mistake, Jim. Please put up with him. It won't be for too much longer."

He didn't answer.

"I think he's sorry enough so that he'll talk to you about a job now. To make it up."

His face was grim. "You have a lot to learn about him." He shrugged. "If I stay, it won't be for the job. I'm not even sure I want to work for him, now. I'd stay for your and Irene's sake."

We went upstairs together. My mind was teeming with Granby's disclosure. What would my mother say? She would never, never believe it of Irene. And poor Uncle Willy, he had always been so proud of his Irene. I wanted to weep for them all.

I stopped at Irene's door to look in on her. Her face was gray in the night light left burning, and her breathing erratic. Once I accepted this reality, the pieces fell into place: her moods of deep depression and weakness, alternating with feverish energy, her inability to eat or sleep, her paranoiac fancies. I had never known anyone intimately who was on drugs, and maybe that was why I had been so slow to recognize the symptoms. But then, so had Jim. Maybe that was because neither of us could believe it of her.

I went back down the corridor toward my room, and almost didn't see Eugene standing in the semidarkness.

"I want to talk to you," he said abruptly. "Can we go to your room?" When he saw me hesitate, he said, "I'll only keep you a minute."

I let him in.

He said, "I never touched her. It's important to me that you know that."

When I couldn't answer—how was I to believe him? —he said, "I heard her moving about her room, talking to herself, and I suspected she'd got hold of the stuff somehow. Mrs. Wall watches her closely, but she manages sometimes, in spite of her. When I opened the door, I startled her. She stepped back and lost her balance. She must have cut her head when she fell. I saw a needle on the floor that she must have dropped when she saw me."

Those thin slivers of glass that Mrs. Wall had mopped up so hurriedly.

"Why didn't you tell me? Why was it kept so secret?"

"She asked me not to tell you. She was ashamed. She couldn't bear for the family to find out."

For a few minutes I could hardly speak. And then I said, "How did it happen?"

"I could tell you a dozen theories. I don't know. Maybe it started in her childhood, making her the kind of woman she is. Maybe it was marriage to me, and the kind of life she led with me. Dissatisfaction with me. Idleness. Boredom."

And that inner circle, waiting with its compensations.

"Even before the drugs, she looked to other men for excitement. She had a lover in the first months we came to Teheran. When I found out, I was still too obsessed with her to want to give her up. I told myself it wouldn't happen again. But it did, again and again. After a while I didn't even keep track. It stopped mattering."

I could say only, "Why did you stay together? Wouldn't it have been better for you both to separate?"

"She was already into drugs. I felt I must see her through, see her cured, and then we could separate. You see, then my obligation to her would be over. I did blame myself, I felt her needing the drugs was somehow due to her marriage to me and going overseas—and so I must help her to get better."

"You made her come here."

"It was a last-ditch effort. Mrs. Wall would watch her, and we were isolated enough so that she'd have no source of supply. And for a while she had none. It was painful, and her health began to go, but I thought she would come through. But then she got hold of the stuff again, I don't know how."

It was so plausible, and I wanted to believe him. "Maybe she doesn't want to be cured," I said, "maybe she knows you'll leave her when she's better."

"But she knows we're finished after this summer! She agreed to that, before we came. This one last attempt, and then, whether she was well or not, she would get a divorce."

I was filled with despair for her, so much that I couldn't speak.

"Look," he said, seizing my hands, "I don't mean anything to Irene. I never did. If I had, would she have needed other lovers? Would she have turned to drugs for satisfaction? My notions of love are probably unsophisticated, and out of date, but I don't believe it could have happened, any of it, if she had loved me enough."

Anything I said now would be wrong, for Irene, for him, for me.

"I'm almost glad you found out," he said. "I think I wanted you to know. When you looked at me tonight I saw on your face the dislike, the distrust, the suspicion that was there in the beginning. I knew then that what you think of me has become very important. It's all that matters, now."

His hands were still holding mine. I pulled them away. "I can't listen to you. You mustn't say any more."

He must have heard the anguish in my voice. "I understand," he said, and went to the door.

I got into bed numbly. Irene was on drugs, and so much of what she said and believed could be fantasy. But not everything; there was enough I'd seen for myself. But no matter what kind of man Eugene was, the man she described or the man I wanted to believe, it could not go any further. I mustn't allow it to go any further.

✿ *11*

*W*hen I looked in on Irene in the morning, she was better. She even dressed and came down to breakfast, and it seemed to me that she had no recollection of last night at all. Her conversation was as usual, and though now and then her fingers would stray to her cheekbone and touch the adhesive tape there, she would only look puzzled, as if it were something she had forgotten, but she didn't bring it up to Jim or me.

She grew increasingly listless during the day, and by late afternoon went to bed. Jim thought it was the drug wearing off, but I thought it was more. She was coughing, and her pale cheeks looked feverish, and when I spoke to Mrs. Wall, she agreed with me that we should have Dr. Granby back. Clarke now stayed at home with us at Skeld House, so he drove into Lerwick to bring the doctor.

Dr. Granby diagnosed it as a viral infection, brought on, no doubt, by her headlong flight across the moor last night in her nightgown. He left pills and suggested she stay in bed until her fever was down.

"She is a poor, sick lady," he said, shaking his head. "It is very sad indeed."

I stayed with her in her room, talking when she seemed to want to talk, reading when she dozed off. And I thought.

My position in Skeld House was now unbearable. Not so much for what had happened between Eugene and me, but for what I was afraid might happen. We were both on our guard, but in spite of that, people in love sense each other's feelings intuitively. He must know my own state of mind just as I knew his. Now was the time to go away, before either of us would be driven into a more open acknowledgment. I reasoned with myself: I may be building on something quite artificial in basis; the fact that we were forced so much into each other's company by loneliness, or his bitterness and frustration in his marriage, or my needing someone to take Dan's place in my life. Real or artificial, it could still be stopped now.

And I forced myself to face painful certainties. Even if Irene had never loved him or had stopped loving him and went on to divorce him, I could never allow our relationship to grow any deeper. Irene would always know that it had begun in this tragic time, and that while I was pretending to help her, I was actually deceiving her behind her back. On the other hand, if she still loved him, and I believed she did, our situation was ugly. It was unthinkable.

I had to go away, the faster the better.

"What is it, Lisette?"

She must have been watching me.

I stammered, "I've . . . been thinking it's . . . time for me to go home."

She cried, "You've only just come!"

"It's been six weeks. I didn't expect to stay this long."

"Lisette, you can't go!"

Her voice was desperate.

"I'm not safe here! I couldn't bear it if you were to go away now!"

I looked away. What could I say, after last night?

Her eyes narrowed, instantly suspicious.

I faltered, "I mean, you said yourself that many of your fears might be due to the accident, that you've been nervous—"

She was always quick to see through me, and I was clumsy when I lied. She lay back. "So he's convinced you."

"No one convinced me of anything."

Her voice could be lifeless as well as seductive. "I can't blame you. People believe Eugene. He manages to seem straight as a die, even when he's lying shamelessly."

"It isn't anything Eugene said, Irene. It's what I know."

"What can you know!" she cried.

I had to tell her then. There was no other way. "I know you take drugs," I said, making myself disregard the look on her face. "It had to come out at some time, and you don't have to be ashamed for me to know." I made myself go on. "I'm so sorry for you, Irene. I know how awful it must be for you. I know how awful you must have felt to be driven to taking them. I want to help you, and I'll do whatever I can, whatever you want, but first you have to face that it's a sickness, and it's why you're afraid and why you have the thoughts you have."

"He told you," she said thinly. "He promised me he wouldn't."

"It was Dr. Granby who told me," I said miserably. "We sent for him last night."

"Granby, our local vet?"

"Irene, what good does that do?"

"What right did he have to tell you? Isn't there such a thing as professional ethics?"

"Irene, I saw you. You ran out of the house, and Jim had to carry you back. You'd fallen and cut your face."

She touched the adhesive patch almost wonderingly, and then her face worked. "It was Eugene! He hates the sight of me! He struck me and knocked me down!" She touched the patch again. "But of course you'll only believe Eugene. Eugene probably bribed Granby to tell you."

I turned away, unable to speak.

She said pitifully, "Why do you believe them and not me?"

"Irene, will you lift your sleeve and let me see your arm?"

She turned her face convulsively and hid it in her pillow.

I went to her and touched her hair. "Irene, it means nothing to me. You're just sick, and you'll have to get well. Irene, listen, come back to the States with me. I'm sure they have places that can help you. It might even be better for you if you were to be separated from Eugene for a while. You might manage to see your own position more clearly—"

"So he could say I'd left him, and divorce me?"

"You agreed to divorce him anyway at the end of the summer."

"No, I won't," she said. "And that's why he wants to have me dead. Or force me somehow to kill myself. Do you know who has been giving me the drugs, Lisette? Eugene. He puts them in my room when I'm asleep. But you wouldn't believe it of him, because he's very charming and very convincing."

I was shocked into silence for a moment, but I reminded myself of her state of mind. "Irene, maybe your whole trouble is guilt, about what happened in Teheran. Maybe if you got away from this atmosphere, you could forget it. You'd be home, and we'd all be with you, your father—"

"My father," she whispered. "I don't want him to know."

"Then he won't know. The only thing you must think about is getting well. Then you can go back to work, modeling, or—"

She laughed bitterly. "Grow up, Lisette. Who would hire me?"

"You're only thirty-two. There's time to start over again."

Her eyes searched me, lit with alarm. "What are you telling me, Lisette? That there's no hope for Eugene and me?"

"How would I know that?" I said wretchedly. "I just think that for now you should go away and be with people who love you."

"And away from Eugene, who doesn't love me. Who slips drugs into my room, so I'll take them and die. Who hires that woman to spy on me and invent lies—"

"Mrs. Wall only watches you to see that you don't take anything."

"Or to see that I do." She lay back on her pillows and looked at me with tired eyes. "I suppose now you'll never believe me. I lied about the drugs. I'm lying about Eugene."

"No, Irene. I do believe you."

"You don't have to deny it. It's there. In your voice. In the way you look at me."

It was useless to pretend.

She said, "I suppose it would be pointless to remind you about the man who broke into the house, who drove away in the van that Jim saw, the van we found. Or about Mrs. Wall, who pedaled out to the van with food, who left our napkin there, whom Eugene is protecting."

Or about the man Eugene spoke to, and denied speaking to. And the man in the shadow of the gardener's shed, lurking, watching. And Eugene's lies. I could have helped her in her accusations.

"Listen," she said. "I know you won't believe me about the drugs, but it's true. I haven't been out of the house in weeks. I got to the stableman once, when we first came, but Mrs. Wall found out, and Eugene fired him. But I find them. In my handbag. In the pocket of my robe.

Eugene puts them there. Or Mrs. Wall. Who else would want to do it? Who else wants to hurt me?"

I couldn't answer.

"Listen," she said again. "You won't believe this, either. You'll say I'm under the influence of a needle, but I'm not, not all the time. It's worse when I'm not. I can't sleep, and sometimes the sedative doesn't help and I jump out of bed and walk up and down half the night until I fall asleep from exhaustion. Sometimes I go to the window and tell myself to jump and make an end of it. But I'm afraid to jump. I'm afraid I won't die, I'll just be crippled. So I stay at the window, staring out, waiting to get the courage. And that's when I see him."

In spite of myself, my skin prickled.

"See whom?"

"You wouldn't believe me if I told you. You'd say I was hallucinating."

"I won't say that."

"Or believe it?"

"I won't believe it, either."

"There's a man who hides outside. I've seen him a few times."

She is lying. She is hallucinating. But I wasn't hallucinating that night. I smelled the presence of a man, I know. And he'd left muddy prints on the sill of my window when he broke in.

I felt cold. Was he lying in wait for her? Or for me?

I said, "What does he look like?"

"I can't tell. He stays in the shadows. He's very good at it. But I have marvelous vision, Lisette, still. He's short, squat, like the man who came into your room to attack me. And sometimes the moonlight strikes his head. He's absolutely bald."

Bald. Like the man who'd spoken to Eugene.

"Have you told Eugene?" I said, carefully.

She laughed at me. "Eugene *knows*, Lisette. He comes out of the house sometimes to meet him, and they talk."

I was struck silent. She was watching me, not as if she had fooled me, but dully, defeated, without hope.

I managed to say, "Then it's all the more reason for you to come away with me."

She turned her head from side to side. "I don't have the strength to make the trip."

"We'll be together, and I'll help you."

She whispered, "Sometimes at night when I see that man and watch Eugene go out to meet him, I want to call out to them, and say, 'You're not tricking me, you're really there, and I see you.' But I'm afraid. Suppose they aren't there? Suppose I just think I see them? Suppose I'm really going mad?"

"You're not going mad. And I'm going to take care of you. I'll even go by plane, if it's easier for you."

She achieved a small, bitter smile. "Then you got something out of this dreadful visit. At least you're better."

"We'll do it in stages, so you won't feel the strain. We'll fly from here to Aberdeen, and rest there a while, and then we'll go on to London and rest some more before we go back to America."

"Do you think it's easy for me, Lisette, to leave him?"

"I know it isn't."

"How will I manage? I need money."

"Eugene will give you the money. Anyway, you don't have to think about money. You could manage for ages on just what that ring would bring."

She said with unexpected passion, "Do you think I'd sell any of it?"

I had no idea her jewelry could mean that much to her. "You don't have to sell it if you don't want to. You won't need to sell it."

She said somberly, "You don't know what it's like, Lisette, to be wildly, extravagantly rich."

"No, I don't."

"It's like being a queen," she said. "People doing everything for you. Nothing you want that you can't have."

Except Eugene.

"How can I go back to the old way?" she said.

"You'll have more than enough. Eugene will see to it."

"You still don't believe he hates me, do you?" She half smiled. "When I go into the divorce court, he'll have all sorts of evidence against me, and I won't get a penny. If I stay with him, I'll have everything."

"Would you stay with him, for that?"

She lifted her shoulders. "But of course it isn't just that."

We stared at one another. I said finally, "Well, whatever you do, I'm going home. I'm going to make my arrangements for Friday. That's almost a week away, plenty of time for you to get over your virus."

She said nothing. I was trying to force her hand.

"I'll make the arrangements for you, too. Just in case you can go. If you don't, they can be canceled. But whatever you do, I'm leaving on Friday."

She turned her face away.

"Will you try and come?"

"I'll try."

I went up to my room to change for dinner.

I was tormented. I had to go, but I knew I did not want to. Even after what she'd told me about the man who lurked outside, watching. It had the ring of truth, and, moreover, it was what I myself suspected; even after that I knew I did not want to leave.

I must make myself see Eugene as the man behind it all. He had confessed to loving Irene excessively; suppose it had turned to the same excessive hatred, so that he wanted to kill her, needed to kill her, uncontrollably. He could afford to buy complicity and silence from some hired assassin. Our coming, Jim's and mine, had complicated his plan, but he could be patient. That night when we'd gone to the Coast Guard Ball had been an opportunity, but we'd aborted it by returning too soon. Maybe he was waiting for us to leave. The assassin could kill Irene and take her jewels as a cover-up; he could vanish easily in a small boat hidden now in some cove. Mrs. Wall would protect Eugene. She was the only servant in the house except for Gerda, who was not overbright and slept soundly. By the time Eugene called the police, the assassin could be well away.

I did not believe it of Eugene.

And all the women who loved unsuspectingly the men

who married them, and murdered them? Did they believe it of the men they loved?

Mrs. Wall was jealous of Irene. She might want to see her beauty destroyed, and might be leaving the drugs for her. She might even be aiding Eugene.

Jim had spoken of Eugene and how he enjoyed using his power. If his anger against Irene was pathological, he might think of himself righteously as her executioner.

Might. *Might.* I couldn't believe it of him. I could not feel the way I did about him if he were a potential murderer. I did not want to go away and never see him again.

I must find out about the man hiding outside the house. I must see him together with Eugene.

I had my dinner with Irene in her room that night, because I could not bear to face Eugene feeling as I did. Jim joined us later, and we worked on a jigsaw puzzle together, until Irene's twitching features and trembling fingers made me glad to see Mrs. Wall enter with her sedation, to get Irene ready for the night.

Jim and I were at the door when Irene called out, "Jim, Lisette is leaving on Friday. Did you know?"

Jim was disconcerted. "No, I didn't."

"She wants me to go with her."

Mrs. Wall was watching us intently.

I said, "We'll talk about it in the morning, Irene."

Out in the corridor Jim said, "Isn't this rather sudden?"

"I can't do anything for Irene," I said. "And staying here is no good for her. She seems to lay her hands on the drugs, somehow, in spite of her isolation. She's only getting worse here."

He agreed thoughtfully. He said, "Well, I might as well pack my things, too. I'm only here to keep you company."

"Do you mind leaving?"

He compressed his mouth. "I haven't worked anything out for myself so far; I suppose I never will."

"About the job, you mean? It's a shame."

"He's an arrogant bastard," he said quietly. "Maybe this business with Irene is what changed him so drastically, but even so, he might have had the decency not to keep me standing around, hat in hand, like some beggar. He owes it to me, damn him, and he knows it."

He stopped when he saw the expression on my face. "Mustn't let it worry you, love. It's my problem." He bent and kissed me lightly on the lips.

I looked up even as he kissed me, and saw Eugene coming up the stairs. He must have seen us, because he went on into his room without speaking.

I felt my face flame.

"Don't mind about his seeing us," Jim said, glancing at Eugene's door as it closed. "After all, he did bring me here to distract you."

I didn't have the time to brood about Eugene catching us in that meaningless kiss. As soon as I closed the door, I began to think about the man outside in the shadows, watching. I discarded immediately the idea that it might be someone after the notes, even though it was the idea that Eugene himself had put forth. If he were after the notes, there would be no complicity between him and

Eugene. It was easier to imagine Eugene as a murderer than a spy. And why should he want the notes? Not for money, certainly. And he had no reason to betray his country. No, I had to know if the man was really there, and then I had to know if Eugene was involved with him.

I couldn't watch from my bedroom because the windows faced north, and if Irene had seen anyone from her room, it would have to be from the south. The drawing room was directly below Irene's room; I could station myself there. I don't know why I didn't tell Jim what I was going to do. I suppose subconsciously I was protecting Eugene. Protecting a possible murderer. I didn't stop to question, incredible as it seems.

I heard Jarvie close the front door and lock it, which meant he would now proceed to his quarters over the garage. The house fell into silence. Was Irene watching from her windows or had the sedative succeeded in helping her to sleep? She'd had a slight fever, and that might make her torpid and drowsier than usual. I waited as long as possible, and then I opened my door a crack and listened.

No sound from any room. I closed my door behind me and, moving very carefully on the stairs so they would not creak, I crept down through the dark hall. The drawing room was dark, too. I made my way in by the gunmetal gray from the outside; even now, in August, a starless night was still not completely black.

Crouching beneath the bank of casement windows to watch, I became aware of a variety of shadows I'd never taken the trouble to notice before. The hedge of shrubs cast an irregular shadow, the roof of the greenhouse a long line, the gardener's shed a tall peaked one. The casement windows were inset with panes of colored glass that were thick and wavy and obscured what view I had. If something moved outside, I might not detect it easily, so, very cautiously, trying not to make a sound, I pressed down on the hinge that latched the window and opened it. Slowly I pushed the frame out, so I could have at least one clear rectangle to see through.

The night air felt clammy and still. The sea seemed especially close, with its smells of salt and seaweed.

What would it be like to breathe the familiar traffic and soot and tar smells of New York streets again? My heart pitched. There was nothing at home anymore for me. My world had transferred itself with unexpected ease to this unfamiliar terrain of rock and moor and peat and water. If Eugene were the reason why, then it was all the more reason to get away, fast.

Irene. Poor Irene. I thought of Mrs. Wall's words. She is her own worst enemy. Even if they had been said with satisfaction or vindictively, they were still true. She'd had everything, as Mrs. Wall had said, and tossed it all away. And why? But Eugene was right, what good did it do to know why. She was the woman a hundred factors had made: the mother who had abandoned her, Uncle Willy, so properly undeviating, so undeviatingly proper, so proud of her, even her beauty, which was how she justified herself, without which she felt worthless, and which needed the constant affirmation of love. How could anyone know what made Irene?

But she was a fact, and I had to accept her as she was. Nothing was unbelievable or impossible to me anymore.

I had learned that much, and that people seek for oblivion and punishment and death as passionately as they seek love. Only a blind, intolerant bigot can't accept the needs and wants of others, no matter how incomprehensible or unreasonable. Eugene was capable of murder, just as I was capable of loving a murderer and denying the facts because I didn't want them to be so.

There was a shadow, different from the others.

My heart lurched, and I strained to see. It was coming toward the shed from the dirt path, keeping to the dappled shadows thrown by the bushes. A man had reached the shed and stood there, waiting, almost invisible, except for the faint sheen from a completely hairless head.

Call Jim. I stood up and ran for the door, pulled it open and bolted across the hall for the stairs.

I crashed into someone hard. A hand went over my mouth, cutting off my breath so that I couldn't make a sound.

"What are you doing down here?"

Eugene. Eugene on his way to meet the man outside.

"What about you?"

He took my arm in a flash of irritation and, holding it firmly so I couldn't shake free, he propelled me back into the drawing room, not letting me go until he had closed the door behind us. When he released me, he went at once to the window and closed it and latched it and then faced me, still in the darkness.

He said, "I saw the window open from my own room and I assumed Jarvie forgot to lock it. I came down myself to shut it."

I didn't believe him.

He said, "With you here, it would be asking for trouble to keep a window open at night."

His voice was entirely steady, but I knew he was lying. Anger filled me, that he could lie so arrogantly. I said, "You know that isn't why you came down."

He lifted his arms and let them fall against his sides. I didn't know if it meant: believe what you want, I don't care, or a helpless futility.

"There's a man outside, and you know who he is."

"You're talking nonsense."

"Irene has seen him, too."

"Irene."

"I didn't entirely believe her either, but I've guessed enough to make me wonder. And so I came to see if he was real. He's there now."

He turned and peered through the glass. "There's no one. See for yourself."

I didn't trouble to look. "Then he was frightened off."

"What did he look like?" he said with elaborate patience.

"He looked like the man you talked to the first night we came, the man you said was Clarke. He's probably the man Irene saw when she went into my room, who you said was Clarke, too. He's probably the man Mrs. Wall met, on the moor, the one she brought food to, on your orders, I'm sure."

"Be quiet, please."

I was talking too loudly in my anger. I didn't want to wake Jim or Irene, and I lowered my voice.

"You've met him, spoken to him. Why do you keep on lying to me?"

He turned away from me and stared through the window, his head and shoulders a defiant dark silhouette against the gray night sky.

"The only man I've met or spoken to out there is the birdwatcher."

"Why do you treat me as if I were a complete fool?"

"Lisette," he said, "the man out there is a birdwatcher. You have to believe me."

I started to laugh, and stifled it.

"Then what is he doing here at night, outside this house? What birds can he watch now?"

"Please believe me," he said. "No matter how ridiculous it sounds."

"I can't believe you. Irene may be in danger. I didn't entirely accept it at first. You managed to convince me she imagined it all. But I can't believe you anymore."

"Listen to me," he said. "The police have questioned him. He's here on a holiday. He's an amateur ornithologist and he's been ranging all over the islands. Fetlar, Foula Cliffs. Not only here. He camps in his van, he rents a boat when he has to. I gave him permission to take what supplies he needs. Gasoline and oil. It's a long way to a filling station. And stuff from the greenhouse. Yes, I did tell Mrs. Wall to bring him some cooked food, and I asked her not to mention it."

"Why? Would Irene refuse to give him any food?"

"You have to trust me, Lisette."

"How can I? If it's true what you say, why didn't you tell us about him from the beginning?"

He took a deep breath.

"Because I know Irene better than you do. Because she

would never have believed me, either. Because she would have been sure it was a plot and that I had brought him here on some purpose of my own, to harm her. You know she's obsessed with the idea that I want to kill her. I could never have made her believe I had nothing to do with him."

"But she's seen him."

"I didn't know that. I've warned him to keep out of sight. He knows about Irene. Lisette, you have to make her think she has only imagined him."

"No, I can't."

"It's for her own peace of mind."

But I remembered something. "He's the same man who broke into the house. She remembers that, too. Short and heavy-set. If he were only a birdwatcher, would he have broken into the house? Or did you give him permission for that, too?"

He said doggedly, "I didn't give anyone permission to break into the house. If anyone broke into the house, it could very well have been someone after your notes. What about the woman at the Royal Hotel? It could have been one of her confederates."

I was silent. There might be some truth to this. Irene may have been too terrified to see the intruder clearly. I said, "Why doesn't he come during the day, then, this . . . birdwatcher? Why is it always late at night? Why is he always hiding?"

"I told you why," he said tightly. "I've mentioned Irene's fear, I've warned him she's ill and that it would be better if she doesn't see him."

I *did* want to believe him, and he *had* produced arguments that were credible, but he said them as if he found what he was saying distasteful, as if there were a bitter taste in his mouth. My head was pounding from the shock of seeing the man outside, from my fright at crashing into Eugene, from anger at his lying.

I said, "I've asked Irene to come back to the States with me when I leave on Friday."

He said sharply, "You're leaving Friday? Why?"

"I don't think I'm needed here. And I think it would be good for Irene to get away as soon as possible."

"As long as she's here, we can watch her closely."

"So closely that she manages to find her drugs as she did last night?"

He was silent for a moment. "I suppose she's more clever at concealing the stuff than we are at finding it."

"I think someone is giving it to her," I said evenly. "Maybe we'll be able to hire someone more reliable to watch her. *If* she comes with me, and I'm still not sure."

"Lisette," he said. "Don't go yet. For my sake."

I shook my head. He probably didn't even see it in the darkness.

He said, "Are you going home because of me?"

I said tightly, "I'm going home because I have to find a job, and because my holiday has lasted long enough."

He followed me when I went to the door.

"Then let me say this much, at least, Lisette. You've helped me see that anything is possible. That I could find a girl and be happy with her when I thought it could never happen to me again—"

"Please, I don't want to hear it," I said, my voice shattering.

He had his hand on the knob. "Let me ask you this, then. If I hadn't been Irene's husband, could you have loved me?"

"I don't want to think about it. I don't know."

"You *have* thought about it. You do know. It's why you're going away."

"Supposing that were my reason, couldn't you see why I have to?"

He didn't answer at once. And then he let go of the knob and said without expression, "Yes, I could see that."

We had taken the step I had been afraid of taking, and now it was expressed, and open. We could only be hurt the more for it.

And there was something else. If he really did love me, and therefore Irene stood in our way, wouldn't this put her in an even more dangerous position in relation to him?

I must make her come with me.

❧ 12

I was to be alone with Eugene only once more before Friday.

On Wednesday he stopped me in the hall as he was leaving for the drilling operations. "I'd like to talk to you."

I suppose I showed my reluctance, because he went on more strongly, "It's important, or I wouldn't insist. We can meet at the works, so you needn't feel afraid. I'll ask Clarke to drive you. And try to think of some story to tell Irene so she won't be suspicious."

I thought, then he's made up his mind to explain what he has been concealing all this time. And I thought, too, I've hurt him by letting him know I don't trust him. Whatever his reasons, it might be best to hear him out.

I made up the story that I felt I should see the operations, since I was leaving on Friday; it would seem strange if I'd been here this long without ever glimpsing them. I told it to Jim at breakfast, and asked him to explain this to Irene when she awoke.

He said doubtfully, "But Eugene told me not to let you go anywhere alone."

"I won't be alone. Clarke is driving me."

It was a gray day, promising more rain. The weather suited my mood. I would not be seeing much more of the Shetlands after today, except for the trip to the airport. Tomorrow would be taken up in packing, not so much my things as the monumental job of Irene's. We hadn't talked any more about her leaving, and I had almost avoided bringing it up for fear she would refuse outright, but I was determined that she must come away with me. She was right when she'd said she could not think clearly: I'd noticed that she could not follow an idea through, and would sometimes change what she'd started out to say as if she'd forgotten the point. I must think for her, difficult as it was. Even if the birdwatcher was there to terrify her, to drive her to taking the drugs, whoever was giving them to her was acting purposefully and cold-bloodedly. Jim and I would manage somehow to get her on the plane. If we succeeded, he would come along with us. If she balked too hard, he would stay behind with her so as not to leave her alone in Skeld House. I no longer had a shred of doubt about coming between her and Eugene: her marriage was over.

The car jolted down the dirt road that had been built by Atico for the drilling. I could see the floating rig from above as we descended, sitting on the water like a long-legged black spider. At the water's edge were the gray sheds and quonsets that served as both offices and living quarters.

Clarke let me out at the gate, but even before I could

walk over to the office that he pointed out, Eugene emerged, as if he'd been watching for me.

"We can walk up here," he said, taking my arm and leading me up the rough path only wide enough to set two feet on. In a moment we were on the top of a headland that protected the cove below. The sound of drilling came to us here, but faintly, a slow, dreary chugging.

He said abruptly, "I asked you to come because it's a kind of goodbye. I find I have to go away tomorrow for several days. I didn't expect I'd have to, but I do."

His words were a blow, and I didn't attempt to reason myself out of admitting it. I had to remember that he was dangerous, that his abrupt departure could be part of his planning, that he was not to be trusted. And yet, in spite of that I did not want to see him go, and even though I was myself leaving on Friday, I had wanted that last day with him.

He said, "There's a summit conference in a hotel in a place called Auchterarder. Most of the companies interested in both North Sea oil and gas are going to be there. Atico will have its representatives, and I didn't think I would have to be there, but it seems I will."

I nodded.

He said, "It's a matter of apportioning areas to the various companies interested. We're not one of the giants, and negotiations will be delicate. We can't afford to be as experimental as some, and we have to be reasonably optimistic about the zones they lease us. My representatives asked me to come."

I nodded again, dumbly.

He said, "I don't like the idea of leaving you at Skeld

House. Clarke will have to fly the plane. I can pilot it myself, but it's easier to have him along."

"I'll be all right. Jim's there."

He seemed to frown.

"There's your gun," I said. "Jim says he's a good shot."

He reached into his pocket and took out the revolver. "I want you to keep it."

I drew back. "I wouldn't know what to do with it."

He said impatiently, "I'll show you." He put the gun in my hand. "It's simple. Release this first, and then press here. Aim as straight as you can. It's loaded."

"I don't think I could ever fire."

"You will if you have to. Put it away where it's safe, and remember, it isn't a game you're playing. That incident at the Royal Hotel was only one episode. It may happen again, and you may not always be as lucky."

I put the gun away in my handbag, which was just large enough to close over it. "I still think it would be better to let Jim have it."

"He might not be with you when you need him, and that's when you'll have to use it." His glance was suddenly very intent. "Are you in love with him?"

I remembered that he had seen us kiss. "No, I'm not."

He hesitated. "Don't get involved with him."

I had no intention of getting involved, but his curt warning put my back up. "Do you have any reason for saying that?"

I thought he would say, because of me, because of us, but he shook his head abruptly.

"Just my judgment, that's all."

"You aren't being fair to Jim to make a statement and leave it without an explanation."

He said with some irony, "You don't trust me. Why should you consider my opinion seriously?"

"At least let me make up my own mind, to be fair to him."

He considered, choosing his words slowly. "He hasn't staying power. He won't stick with anything. He'll lose interest fast."

"You're thinking of his leaving Atico. But that was only after he tried desperately to be placed in a job he was fitted for."

"He told you that." He thought. "Jim's ambitious, yes. But he wants to be rewarded for his father's service to the company rather than for his own. His father was paid in stock for his invention, and it would have made him rich if he had held on to it, but he sank it into experiments that failed. Jim blames us. He wants to be pushed up fast because of that, and not because he's earned his promotions."

I spoke carefully. "Are you . . . being objective about him? Isn't he acting like any man anxious to get ahead?"

"I have the judgments of the men he's worked under." He was plainly impatient to end talk of Jim. "Look, right now it's you I'm concerned about. You're just getting over a tragic experience. I don't want to see you tie up with someone who may hurt you."

"I didn't really have any intention of getting tied up with him."

He said, "I'm glad."

I thought it best to move the conversation away from me. "I think Irene is actually coming with me. And it may be just what she needs, to find herself in a completely new environment. Maybe that will help her put whatever happened here out of her mind."

"She won't go," he said. "She's grown to need the kind of life she's led with me."

"The kind of life she led pushed her toward drugs. What she really needs, and wants, is for you to love her."

Even to express the thought filled me with despair.

"You mustn't let yourself believe that, Lisette. Irene is a sick woman. She was never capable of love."

It was a cruel and painful statement to accept, and he read that on my face. He went on urgently, "I know you don't want to believe it. But I've lived with her. I know her as you can't ever know her."

He was so utterly convincing. I was convinced again.

"Whatever she told you, she knows she must start divorce proceedings this fall, or I will. She knows I will provide her with whatever she needs. Lisette, you mustn't let Irene stand between us!"

My intelligence accepted what he told me. A divorce was inevitable. What reason could he have to see her suffer, or to want her dead? Unless I did not know him, unless he is sick, unless he is concealing a pathological hatred under his quiet manner.

And there was something else, too. Unless he has made me love him for his own purposes, seducing me so that I cannot see him for the man he is. So that I might refuse to see him for what he was just as he had refused to see Irene for what she was after finding her with her lover.

200

I forced myself to see his face, as if I could wrench the truth from him. We stared at one another mutely. And then, tentatively, he reached out his hand and touched my hair.

"Your hair is wet."

He smoothed it back, surer of himself as I stood and let him. His hands cupped my face, and he put his mouth on mine. I kissed him. In a day I wouldn't see him again. This moment was all I would take from Irene, if it were hers to give anymore. I would always remember it as painful, if that could appease my conscience, more painful than I could bear.

He held me as we walked back to the car, almost as if he knew how hopeless it all was. "I'll be at the Gleneagles, in Auchterarder, if you need me."

I repeated the name of the hotel.

Silently I got back into the car, and Clarke came from one of the sheds and drove me back to Skeld House.

I ran upstairs and closed my door. My face stared at me from the mirror, twisted in misery, wet hair plastered to my cheeks, skin beaded with drops, eyelashes stuck together in dark points as if I had been crying.

It wasn't as if I were blind to the kind of man he was. It wasn't as if I were taking anything from Irene.

Hopeless, said my conscience. Even if he were blameless, you could never be happy with him. Never.

❧ 13

*E*ugene left in the morning. He breakfasted with Jim and me, and was equally impersonal with both of us. I expected the constraint between him and Jim, which had existed since the flare-up between them over Irene, but I wondered that he could be as remote to me after our meeting, and our kiss.

He turned to Jim as he left. "Will you be here when I get back?"

"I'm not sure," Jim said briefly. "Only if Irene wants me to stay."

Clarke was waiting for him, to drive him to Sunburgh and the airfield there. Either Clarke or Eugene would pilot the plane; both were licensed to fly. As he turned to go, he looked back at me from the car. I thought I read something in his glance, but maybe it was because I was looking for it.

Irene came down the stairs as the car drove away. Her face was set. "He never told me he was leaving, not until this morning! He's up to something! I know it!"

"The conference seems very important, Irene, or he wouldn't go."

She turned on me. "Then why did he keep it a secret?"

"He didn't plan on going, until the last minute."

Her eyes were sharp, suddenly. "Did he tell you that? I didn't know he was in the habit of confiding in you."

"Come on, Irene," Jim said gently, "that's hardly a confidence."

"He has a reason for going. You'll see. You think I'm neurotic or crazy, but I know."

"Irene," I said, "why don't we go up to your room and start getting some things together. You'll take just what we can carry on the plane, but you can pack whatever you'll need to be sent along after you."

She looked disconcerted.

"You're coming with me. Tomorrow, Irene, remember."

"I can't," she said. "I told you, I can't." She looked to Jim desperately, as if for help.

"I think it's a good idea," Jim said. "It'll just be for a while, and then you can come back."

"Come back?" she cried. "You know he won't take me back! I won't leave him! No!"

"Irene, you said you were afraid to stay here."

"I am." Again she looked imploringly at Jim, as if he could solve her predicament.

He said quietly, "Go with Lisette, Irene."

She stood irresolutely.

"Is the luggage in the storeroom, where Mrs. Wall put mine?" Jim asked.

"I suppose so," she said, frowning.

"I'll tell her to bring it along to your room, Irene," he said. "And yours and mine, too, right, Lisette?"

I nodded. When he'd left us, I made her come to the drawing room and sit down in front of the fire with me.

"I feel sure it's the right thing," I said. "You know I wouldn't urge you, otherwise."

She lifted her shoulders and let them fall as if she were tired. "So much you don't understand, Lisette. I don't know anymore, myself. I don't know what's happening. It's all so confusing."

"We'll find the best doctors—"

She gripped my arm. "Remember, my father isn't to know!"

"He doesn't even have to know you're back if you don't want him to. We can wait until you're better. You'll stay with me for a while. And you'll leave a note for Eugene, I'll help you write it, telling him to keep your going home secret, to arrange something about your mail, for your father."

"You seem to think he gives a damn about helping me. You *are* a fool, Lisette, letting him blind you."

"If he isn't interested in helping you, then it's all the more reason for you to get away."

I knew there was no use fighting her fears, and that it was easier to play along with them. Even if she was all wrong, even if Eugene's account of the birdwatcher was true, it no longer mattered once I got her on the plane, and I would gain nothing by trying to persuade her that a story I didn't believe myself was true.

After lunch I managed to get her to lie down and rest, telling her I would be in later so she could tell me what she wanted me to pack. It would be a tedious job, because she had traveled with trunks, and she would never be able to cope with decisions about her wardrobe. My own packing could wait till later that night: I'd only the valise and an overnight bag with me.

I saw her upstairs, covered her with a light throw, and hoped she would sleep. I wanted to talk to Jim about tomorrow, how we could handle our departure, and what we would do if she suddenly changed her mind and resisted.

We walked out together even though it was drizzling again. I needed the fresh air. It was good for me that I was so taken up with Irene and the preparations for leaving, otherwise my despondency might have been more than I could conceal. We talked quietly, and he suggested that Mrs. Wall give Irene a tranquilizer in her coffee in the morning. The plane left at eleven, which meant that a pill would carry her over at least until we were in Aberdeen, and by that time she might be more resigned.

I said, "Eugene wants me to have his gun."

He stopped in his tracks. For a second his face was blank. "Why?" he said. He recovered. "You don't even know how to use it, do you?"

"He showed me. I'm sure I'd never be able to pull the trigger, but he said I should keep it with me at all times."

"I don't understand why he gave it to you," he said slowly.

"He thinks I'm in danger. That woman who came to the Royal Hotel. He thinks there may be others."

"I suppose he's right," he said. "I hadn't thought of it

that way, not as long as you're here in Skeld House, with all of us around."

"There was that man who broke in."

"True," he said thoughtfully. "I suppose I'm less and less convinced that the man wasn't really after Irene, as she says. There has to be some reason for her feeling about Eugene as she does."

"Why should he risk everything to have Irene killed? Why, when he can be rid of her without any trouble in the courts in a few weeks? When even if she refuses to divorce him, he can divorce her. He has all the evidence he needs!"

It made sense. I wanted to believe it.

"Because I see the embittered, hostile man he's become. I knew him before, remember, and I can see how he's changed. Because he's ruthless, he can't bear to be treated as she treated him, and he thinks he's powerful enough to get away with it. He's not thinking sanely either, remember. He wants to get back at her in the worst way."

I thought of his kiss and the way he had spoken to me. "I don't believe he's insane, Jim. Or even sadistic."

He stopped to study me for a moment, and I felt my face redden under his searching glance.

"You like him, rather."

"I don't trust him, Jim, completely; I know he's concealing something, I know he's lying, I know how bad he's been for Irene, but—"

"But you do like him."

"What does that mean, Jim?" I tried to speak calmly.

He began to smile. "It means I've noticed that he likes you too. And don't be upset, because why shouldn't you both have a nice regard for each other? It's perfectly natural. I just happened not to be aware of it."

"Jim, do we have to talk nonsense now? We have to think about how we're going to handle tomorrow."

"Right on," he said. "Only, I'm beginning to see the light about a few things. Such as why I never got to first base with you—"

I didn't have to search for an answer. Gerda appeared at the kitchen door, and when she spied us, she came running.

"Mrs. Wall!"

Before she got her breathless words out, I had a nightmare vision of Mrs. Wall doing something horrible to Irene. But it wasn't that at all.

"Mrs. Wall had a bad fall, and she's in terrible pain!"

We hurried back to the house, Gerda filling in the details. Mrs. Wall had gone to the store closet to take down the luggage from the shelves. A set of wooden steps was kept there for that purpose, but while she was reaching for the valises the step had given way and Mrs. Wall had crashed down backward.

"Jarvie and I, we got her to her bed, but she's in terrible pain."

"You have a look, Lisette," Jim said. "I'll call Granby."

I ran upstairs to the floor above our bedrooms where her room was. She was lying on her bed, twisted in an awkward position, as if she couldn't straighten herself out. Her face was fixed in a grimace.

"Mr. Baird is calling Dr. Granby."

"Jarvie has already called him."

She could hardly get the words out, her lips were so compressed with pain.

"Can I get you something? Some aspirin, until Dr. Granby comes?"

She nodded, and gestured with her head toward the bathroom in the hall. I found the aspirin in her cupboard, and brought it to her with a glass of water. She could not move, only lifting her head a little so as to swallow the pill.

"Can I help you lie flat?"

She shook her head. "I can't. I believe it's my back. It may be broken."

"Oh, no! Sprained. Or wrenched. That can be terribly painful, too."

She shook her head. "Broken, I think." She fixed her pale eyes on me. "It was done on purpose."

"Oh, no, Mrs. Wall! It couldn't be!"

"Those steps." She stopped and caught her breath, as if she couldn't sustain the effort of talking. "They're sturdy as a rock. They've been in the house . . . and they are made to last for a century. I weigh very little. Jarvie says . . . the wood had splintered."

I could only stare.

"*She* did it," Mrs. Wall said. "She is mad, Mrs. Farrar is. She hates me, and I've never harmed her except to do my job."

"She couldn't have done it. I was with her, and then she went to sleep—" She could have stolen out of her room while Jim and I were out walking. But where would she get the energy to split the wood and put it back together again? Yet I had seen her muster unlikely spurts of energy.

Jim came up, and motioned me to come out into the hall.

"Granby is on his way, and an ambulance, too. Jarvie told him she may have broken her back."

"Does Irene know?"

"Her door is closed, and I didn't want to disturb her if she's sleeping. But she may have heard the commotion."

We left Gerda to stay with Mrs. Wall, and I went down to Irene's room. Her door was always unlocked, and now I understood why her side of the connecting doors to Eugene's room was kept unlocked, too. She was not allowed keys to her room, for fear of what she might do behind locked doors.

I did not want to waken her, either, if she was sleeping, so I noiselessly opened the door a crack just wide enough to look in.

She was awake.

"What happened? I heard a lot of running about."

I couldn't figure out if she were only pretending ignorance or not. "Mrs. Wall fell and hurt her back. We've sent for the doctor."

She said nothing, not even a word of regret. A small twist of her mouth was all, too brief for me to try to understand what it meant. It was unlike Irene to be cruel and vindictive. I could only imagine how distorted Irene's world had become, with its secret enemy and ever-lurking danger.

Dr. Granby came, and went up at once to see Mrs. Wall.

"She'll have to go to Lerwick for X-ray examination," he told us. "Even if it turns out to be nothing serious, we will probably keep her in bed for a few days until she is out of pain and able to walk."

Two men came with a stretcher and blankets and managed to lift her onto it and carry her down to the ambulance. We watched her driven away. Dr. Granby had stopped in to speak to Irene before he left, and while he was with her I looked for the cook to tell her not to fix anything elaborate for dinner. I found her in the kitchen with her hat and woolen cardigan on, even though it was not yet five o'clock and she always stayed until eight.

"I've left you a roast in the oven, and potatoes in a pot," she said. "I must be getting home early today."

"That's all right," I said. "Gerda and Jarvie will serve."

"Jarvie will have to serve by himself," she said a little grimly. "Gerda is driving back to Lerwick with the doctor."

I cried, "Why?"

"Because she isn't safe in this house with a madwoman."

"That's ridiculous!" I cried. "Mrs. Farrar is ill, not mad, and she wouldn't hurt anybody!"

"Wouldn't she, now," said the cook. "And how do you account for Mrs. Wall's accident?"

"The step broke, that was all—"

"Sawed through," said the cook. "Jarvie found the

shavings wrapped in a newspaper on the cold hearth in Mrs. Farrar's room."

Gerda came in then, looking shamefaced, carrying a valise.

"Gerda, you're not really leaving."

"You won't be needing me after tonight," she said, avoiding my eyes. "You'll all be gone in the morning."

"But *why?*"

She looked to the cook, as if for support. "Don't like it here, with Frank Clarke gone and all," she muttered.

"But we're here, Mr. Baird and I. And Jarvie. What can possibly happen?"

"I canna tell for sure," she said. "Only she's real queer, Mrs. Farrar. And if Mrs. Wall's back is broken, I'll know who it is to blame."

There was no point in arguing. As she said, we wouldn't care, after tonight, and I was sure Eugene and Clarke would get her to return, with the cook, once they were back and Irene was gone.

Dr. Granby was waiting in the hall for Gerda. When she appeared behind me, he motioned her abruptly to go out to his car.

"The girl's a fool, but I won't stop her if she wants to go, and she has asked me for a ride to town. Mrs. Farrar will be leaving with you in the morning?"

"I hope so." I said slowly, "Dr. Granby, is there a cure for her?"

He hesitated. "She will have to want to cure herself first. Only then."

🌿 *14*

Only why should she want to be cured, now? Everything that mattered to her was being abandoned, lost forever to her. I couldn't even be sure she would ever be well again physically, enough to start building a life all over again.

But leaving here was a beginning as well as an ending, and I had to make sure she came with me. When I went up to her room she was still in bed where I'd left her.

I forced a briskness I did not feel. "Here I am, ready to help you pack. Let's get it over with as fast as we can, so you can get enough rest for the trip tomorrow."

She didn't answer, but at least she didn't say no.

Several valises stood in a corner of her room. I picked out two of the largest. "These should do."

She shrugged. "It's hopeless. There are trunks and trunks upstairs, and I haven't even looked in them. I suppose I ought to take just what's in these wardrobes." She forced herself to get up, and, going to one armoire, she gathered an armload of dresses and flung them on the bed. "Call Gerda," she said. "Mrs. Wall usually does the packing, but Gerda can help."

I hesitated. But she would find out at dinner that Gerda was gone, so I might as well tell her now. "Gerda went home with Dr. Granby," I said casually. "She said we'd be leaving in the morning anyway and wouldn't need her, so she'd go with him."

She stood still a long moment, while I pretended not to see the surmise on her face. "So she's gone, too," she said.

I tried to disregard her comment. "Irene, all these long things? Couldn't some of them be sent on?"

She said quietly, "You know what it means."

"Irene, this sequinned thing, for instance—"

But I couldn't distract her. "Mrs. Wall is gone. Gerda is gone. There's only Jarvie left."

"And Jim. And me," I said firmly. "And Nichols is around somewhere."

"Nichols is old, and can't even hear. And Jarvie would run for his life at the first threat of danger. Eugene arranged it, going off and taking Clarke with him. Who is going to protect us now?"

"We have the gun, Irene," I said. "By tomorrow we'll be out of Skeld House. Eugene knows that. He knows you're going to get your divorce. What possible reason could he have to stop you now?"

"He doesn't want to see me escape from here. From him."

She meant every word. I was heavy-hearted. "Irene, Jim and I are going to watch you, and see that you're safely on the plane in the morning. You mustn't be afraid anymore."

She lifted her shoulders and let them fall helplessly, her mouth twisted at my refusal to see her danger. But she did begin to empty drawers, pushing underwear of the most delicate crepe and chiffon helter-skelter into the valise. She opened an alligator case that held her jewelry, and I was amazed at the quantity and at the size of the stones in so many of the pieces. She handled them almost reverently.

"This was designed for me in Paris, when we were first married. This is from that man in Athens, Chryso— something or other, these are from Bulgari, in Rome, this is Schlumberger." She held them up against her as she talked. "You should have seen how I looked in them once. What a travesty."

"All you need is care, and you'll be yourself again—"

It was late before we closed and locked the luggage and went to dinner. The dining room seemed too shadowy, too empty without Eugene's presence, without even Gerda's, hovering about the table. We had our coffee, and Irene rose almost at once.

"I'm going up. What time shall we meet in the morning?"

Jim and I looked at each other. He said, "The plane is at eleven. Takes about an hour and a half to drive down. I think we should all be having breakfast by eight-thirty."

She left us.

Jim said, "I think she's going to go after all. If she can."

"What do you mean by that? She seems all right."

"I don't like this business about Mrs. Wall. And Gerda going. Something may be up. You have the gun?"

"Don't tell me you're being as morbid as Irene."

He said slowly, "He decided rather suddenly to go. Right after you said you were leaving."

I was taken aback. "But the conference—"

"You don't understand, Lisette. Eugene doesn't have to be there any more than he does here. He's got the best brains to represent the company, legal and political as well as scientific. Could it be only coincidence that he's managed to be away from Skeld House now, now that he knows you're leaving on Friday? And Mrs. Wall's accident. Could it be only coincidence?"

"He wasn't even here—He didn't know Mrs. Wall would go and fetch the luggage—"

"Mrs. Wall always fetches the luggage and packs for Irene and for whatever guest is here, and Eugene knows it. He could have broken the rung and fitted it together and planted the shavings in Irene's room to make it look as if she'd done it."

He watched me soberly.

"You have the gun?"

"In my handbag, on the shelf in my closet. Why would he give me his gun?"

"He may have another. He may know you wouldn't know how to use it, whereas I would. Probably told you not to tell me you had it."

"No."

"Well, just giving it to you might allay your suspicions. As it seems to."

Jarvie came out into the front hall, ready to leave, and

Jim called to him to make sure all the doors and windows were locked. I went into Irene's room to see if she was all right.

She was sitting in the deep armchair near the fire, her face working, her fingers pulling at each other.

"Can't you sleep?"

"Mrs. Wall has my tranquilizers. In her pocket."

I was aghast.

Just when Irene needed all the rest she could get for the trip tomorrow. And to make her quiescent enough to go with us.

"Would aspirin help? Jim has some."

She shook her head. "Aspirin doesn't help me. *He* wants it this way, so I'll be too upset to travel."

"I'll stay with you. We'll talk until you fall asleep."

"You have to pack your own things."

I had told her I'd save my packing for tonight. "Tell you what. I'll bring you some hot milk, and that may get you drowsy."

I ran down to the dark kitchen and heated up some milk for her and brought it to her; she drank it and then meekly got into bed. I left her, promising to look in again as soon as I'd finished.

Jim's door was open, and I could see him packing, too. He shrugged. "I never thought the holiday would be such a bust, did you? Well—how's Irene?"

"Mrs. Wall went off with her tranquilizers. I hope she gets some sleep. I've given her hot milk to drink."

"She'll quiet down. And I think she's convinced she may as well leave, which will make it easier."

My own packing was negligible, but somehow it's always harder to fit things back a second time than it is the first. I found myself taking bulky sweaters out and refolding them and smoothing them down as carefully as when I'd put them in fresh from the cleaners. It was while I was folding and refolding one skirt that I felt the rustle of paper.

The skirt was a knit jersey, with a lining. The rustle of paper came from down around the hem. I remembered: this was the skirt with a hole in the pocket that everything fell through. Everything fell through it and was caught in the lining.

My arms and legs were numb.

This was the suit I'd been wearing that day when the telegram came telling me Dan was dead.

I already knew what I would find, what that rustle of paper meant.

With numb fingers I reached down through the hole in the pocket into the lining, and there at the hem I touched a piece of paper, and drew it out.

It was blue, faded from cleaning fluid, but still blue. My mother. She had come to my room those first frantic terrible days, and, in her zeal to be helpful, had carried the suit home to be cleaned. She might even have found it rumpled on the floor where I had kicked it that blind night when I'd staggered back to the apartment from my trip to the Copper Kettle Inn. She had probably forgotten about it herself, and had only returned it when I'd needed some warm clothes for the trip.

My hands still thick and wooden, I carried the notes to the lamp. Except for a faint blurring, the notes were decipherable. And dangerous.

What to do. I tried to think. Call Beale? I couldn't reach him in the middle of the night. Cable? A cable was too public. Someone might be watching. I'd be home in a few days. But were a few days too long, might not a few hours be important?

That was when I thought of Eugene. Eugene would have the means to get the information to Larris Foundry without anyone knowing. There was no reason to imagine that anyone would be watching him. I thought: call right away. He won't be in bed, and even if he were, this was an important enough reason to wake him. Where to put the notes meanwhile? They'd been safe all this while in the hem of my skirt. But suppose someone were to break in tonight and go through my luggage? I had no time to think it through,I knew only that I wanted the notes on me. I changed out of the dress I was wearing, putting it in my valise, and put on the skirt with the notes in it, and the jacket. I would travel in it tomorrow.

I can't explain why I wanted to tell only Eugene. Maybe I thought the fewer who knew the better. I left my room quietly and went down to the kitchen to use a telephone where I would not be overheard.

I asked to speak to Auchterarder, and gave the operator the name of the Gleneagles Hotel. I would not mention the notes openly, I would ask him if he would call my office in New York to tell them I'd be coming back to work, everything had been cleared up, cryptic words that I was sure he would understand, as well as the need for secrecy.

The kitchen was large and shadowy. Through its un-curtained windows I could see the stables and the garage;

they were dark, which meant that Jarvie was asleep. The house was unnaturally quiet. I thought of the bird-watcher. Suppose I were to see him now, moving into the shed for gasoline, into the greenhouse for food, stealthily, so that Irene should not discover him. Could I still believe, as I had that night when Eugene had pressed my hands in his, that he was only a birdwatcher?

"Gleneagles Hotel. May I help you?"

The voice was startlingly close.

"I'd like to speak to Mr. Eugene Farrar, please."

"Just one moment."

The moment stretched endlessly. I kept my eyes turned away from the window, where an unexpectedly clear moon shone whitely on the grounds. If the bird-watcher were there, in spite of Eugene's assurance, I did not want to see him.

"I'm sorry. Mr. Farrar isn't in his room. If you'll wait, I'll have him paged in the hotel."

"Yes, please." Nervously I fingered the notes in my skirt. I should have been relieved about them; I felt only apprehension.

"I'm sorry. He doesn't seem to be in the hotel or on the grounds." Pause. "Will you leave a message."

My throat felt very dry. "Yes. Tell him Lisette Knowles called. To please call back as soon as he can."

"Lisette—Did you leave a message earlier?"

"No—"

"Hmm," said the voice. "It's an odd name, French, isn't it? I could have sworn I took a message for Mr. Farrar from someone by that name. It caught my eye somehow. Well. I'll see that he gets the message at once, as soon as he comes in."

I hung up, standing uncertainly in the kitchen. What to do with the notes? I was afraid to go to bed, or to sleep. And I didn't want anyone else to hear the telephone. The best thing might be to station myself down here in the kitchen where I wouldn't be seen, where I could pick up the telephone at once. If I caught it on the first ring it was hardly likely that Jim or Irene would hear it behind their closed doors.

The first thing I must do is take the gun downstairs and keep it beside me. I might not be able to fire it, or even aim it properly, but it might serve as a deterrent to anyone who forced his way in.

I made my way noiselessly back to my room. The luggage still yawned on my bed, half packed; I had forgotten that I hadn't finished the job. It would have to wait until the morning. I went to the closet for my bag and opened it. The gun was gone.

I tipped the bag over on the bed in frantic haste and shook it. But there was no mistake, and I knew it: the gun was too solid and heavy to get caught even in the still torn lining. I pulled a chair over to the closet and searched the shelf where I'd put the handbag, in case it had fallen out. I searched the floor, and among the things I had already packed. It wasn't there. I couldn't have lost it. Someone had taken it.

It was then that I must have stopped thinking clearly. My heart was pumping hard, a thousand thoughts, half formed, whirred in my head, one giving way to the other so fast I could not follow them through: the notes, Eugene, the gun—I was in danger. The notes were in danger. Get Jim.

Get Jim.

I let myself out of my room, still remembering that I mustn't wake Irene. It was important that she get through the night, for tomorrow. I tapped on his door lightly, but he didn't answer. He was asleep. If I knocked louder or called out, I would wake Irene. Quietly I tried the knob; the door was unlocked, and I opened it a crack.

"Jim?"

I went up to his bed. The bed was empty.

"Jim!" I whispered urgently. The bathroom door was open and dark.

The panic that had begun grew. The room seemed suddenly ominous. Was someone hiding here, watching me? I could almost hear breathing, feel eyes piercing the darkness. I ran out again.

Irene.

Dear God, Irene.

I ran down the hall. Mustn't wake her if she's sleeping. Mustn't let her see my terror. I turned her knob softly, somehow managing to control my shaking fingers so that I made no sound as I opened her door—

The figure on the bed half rose, separated, became two.

I stood frozen. A thought came to me, Eugene is back, he has attacked her. A faint light came from a lamp in the dressing room. Irene sat up, drawing the sheet up to her. Jim sprang off the bed, and reached for a robe.

I turned, shut the door behind me, ran to my room and locked the door.

A blankness settled over my mind, as if it wanted to reject what I had seen, as if it were too stunned to accept it. I even began to finish packing, like a machine that has been programmed to do a job and cannot stop, empty this, fold that, buckle and clasp—

Someone was knocking on my door. Jim. He called me. "Lisette, I have to talk to you."

"It can wait till morning. I must finish packing."

"It's important, for Irene's sake, or I wouldn't insist."

I unlocked the door and let him in.

He said, "I don't want you to believe things about Irene that aren't true. I don't give a damn what you want to believe about me, but at least understand Irene. She went looking for you, she was scared, and she was even more scared when you weren't in your room. So she knocked on my door, shaking and whimpering, and I took her back to her room and put her into bed and told her it was all right, that you'd probably gone downstairs to the kitchen for something to eat."

"You don't have to explain," I said dully. "It isn't any of my business."

"But it is," he said. "Irene cares what you think of her, and it will be terrible for her if you don't realize what happened. She clung to me like a frightened child, Lisette, that was all. I comforted her, I held her for a little while until she quieted down. That was all, I swear, and for her sake at least, believe it."

"Please, it's all right. You don't have to tell me. I only came to her room because you weren't in yours, and I couldn't find the gun, and then, when I saw the notes—"

"What?" he said, stopping me short. "What notes? *Beale's notes?*"

"I found them. When I was packing. I didn't know I had them. I couldn't call New York in case anyone was listening on the line. I tried Eugene, and when he was out, I didn't know what to do—"

The words poured from me incoherently. His face was a blank as he listened. And then he collected himself.

"Lisette, lock your windows and door and stay in your room. Under no circumstances leave it, hear me?"

I nodded, dumbly.

"I'll patrol the house, outside as well as in. No one will be able to get past me, and if I see anyone, I'll be ready for him. You're not to worry. Try and get some sleep. You and Irene are perfectly safe. Remember, *don't unlock your door for anything. Or anybody!*"

I nodded.

He left me, and I locked the door behind him.

I finished packing and closed the big valise, leaving the small one open for my last-minute things. I thought of Irene. How could she sleep? How humiliated she must feel! I had to look in on her, at least to tell her it was all right and that I understood.

I opened my door quietly and listened. No sound. Jim must be outside. I hurried down the hall to Irene's room and tapped on the door.

"It's me. Lisette."

"Come in."

Her voice was colorless, spent. She lay neatly in the center of her bed, the way a child's doll is placed to sleep. Her eyes were open.

I said, "I just wanted to make sure you were all right."

"I'm glad you know about us, Lisette," she said. "I didn't want to lie to you about Jim, but he warned me we had to keep it a secret because of the divorce. We've been lovers since Teheran."

Jim had lied to protect her, of course. Irene was speaking the truth. They had both been naked, in bed.

"When he knew Eugene was bringing me here, Jim wanted to come. But he couldn't. Eugene wouldn't let me have company. Eugene hates me and wants me dead. Or at least sick. Or mad. Jim cares for me, loves me. I do need someone, Lisette. When I wrote Jim and told him you were coming, he wrote back and said I should tell Eugene I wanted to invite someone for you. And as Jim said, Eugene had to agree."

My tired mind was trying to absorb her words. Jim had lied, even about his feelings for me. He had to. He had to protect Irene. Of course.

"You think I'm horrible, don't you?" she whispered.

"I don't at all, Irene."

"You do. I can see it on your face. You have to understand, Lisette, how dreadful it's been for me. Gene so cold and hateful, and vengeful. I felt ugly, hideous. I do need someone to love me, and make me feel human again."

She was crying, the tears running silently into her pillow. I found a tissue and wiped her cheeks.

"Don't think about it anymore. Tomorrow we'll go away, and this nightmare will be over."

"I did want you to come, Lisette. Do you believe me? It wasn't just as an excuse to have Jim here. I didn't even think of that until he told me. He said it was a way for him to be with me, that Eugene would buy it. But I did want you here. I wanted you here before he suggested it."

"I know. Don't worry about it."

"You see, I'm so afraid of Eugene."

"There's nothing to be afraid of anymore. Jim's watching the house, and by tomorrow we'll be safely away from here."

She seemed calmer when I left her. I hurried down the quiet hall to my room and locked the door again. I didn't want to undress; I wanted the notes on me, close to me. Besides, I felt less vulnerable in my clothes, and so I lay down as I was. I thought I would drop off to sleep at once out of exhaustion, but instead, disjointed thoughts raced through my head.

Inexplicably, I saw Jim's face as I told him about the notes, and the gun, I saw it more clearly than I had at the time, when I'd been so overexcited. It had been guarded and without expression. Almost as if he hadn't been surprised, as if he had suspected all the time that I had the notes. As if he had known all the time the gun was gone.

As if he had known all the time the gun was gone.

But how could he? Unless . . . unless he had taken it.

I tried to find some logical, innocent reason why he should have taken the gun. He had felt it would be useless in my hands, that he at least knew how to fire it.

He had lied about being Irene's lover. I tried to find a logical, innocent reason for that, too. He had to protect Irene. Irene was going to divorce Eugene. If Eugene knew about Jim, it would only make things worse for her in the proceedings.

226

Who had called Eugene at the Gleneagles Hotel tonight and left a message supposedly from me? It could
only be a ruse. To get Eugene to come back, unexpectedly, and surprise Irene and Jim together? To give him
a reason to kill them both? But who would send it, who
would gain? Unless Eugene sent the message to himself.
Or had had Clarke or Mrs. Wall do it for him. When a
man's home is violated, wasn't that sufficient justification
for clemency, in a crime of passion?

In my anxiety, I could no longer lie still in bed. I
jumped up and began to pace. I drew aside the drapes and
pressed my hot face against the cold glass.

That was how I saw Eugene come silently across the
grass to Skeld House. Stealthily, like an assassin.

✾ 15

A crime of passion. Killing his wife and her lover in his own home would justify a husband's act in the eyes of a jury. Temporary insanity. He had waited for an opportunity to be called away, so he could return unexpectedly.

Only I couldn't believe it. He didn't love or hate Irene that much anymore, so that he would be driven to murder. He loved me. Unless I were an utter fool, he loved me.

Then why was he here?

A message had brought him here, a message signed in my name. It couldn't have been my message that had brought him back; my message wouldn't have been received in time so that he could drive to the airport, fly here, land in Sunburgh, and drive to Skeld House, not in so short a time. It was that other message that had brought him back, a false message.

Someone wanted him here. Someone was plotting to

bring him back, ostensibly in answer to a message from me. Why?

The front door closed heavily behind him. I could hear it even behind my door. Where was Jim? Jim was supposed to be patrolling the house. If he had not seen Eugene approach, he must have heard the sound of the closing door. Why didn't he confront him? It would have been only natural to have spoken to him, if he'd seen him, ask him what had brought him back so unexpectedly.

Unless Jim had expected him. Unless Jim had sent the message to bring him here. But why?

The answer pierced my mind as clear and sharp as a sliver of broken glass. No time to be sure, to follow my own reason, to see if it held: my instinct guided me. I *knew.*

Already I could hear the stair treads give under Eugene's feet. I tugged at the door frantically until I remembered that I had locked it under Jim's instructions. Unsteady in my feverish haste, I managed to wrench it open, and plunged out into the dark hallway.

Eugene stood in the light from Irene's opened door. "No!"

My voice screamed the warning, but it was too late. I heard the shot, and saw him reel against the doorjamb.

Irene was crying wildly, "I told you I couldn't!"

"You fool," said Jim's furious voice. "You blew it!"

I rushed forward to see them together, Jim and Irene. I saw Jim take the gun from Irene's limp hand and fire again directly at Eugene. Blood poured from Eugene's neck and dyed his collar red. He doubled over on himself and fell forward.

I reached toward him futilely. Irene said over and over again, "Eugene. You killed him." She clawed at Jim, trying to wrest the gun from him, while Jim held her away, but her hand closed over the gun. He was still holding it when she pressed it, and the third shot rang out. Irene slumped to the floor.

Jim stared at her, transfixed, and then slowly his stunned, blank eyes came around and found me. He came toward me, mechanically, as if he didn't know what he was going to do. I could not move.

Jim lifted his hand, the gun still in it.

My voice breathed, "No," even as there was a shattering pain in my head, and then nothing.

✱ 16

I opened my eyes to utter blackness. I was aware of damp stone, and cold. I thought, I'm buried alive.

I think I shouted, and cried, before I lapsed into unconsciousness. When I opened my eyes again I knew it was no dream; strangely, I was still alive.

Cautiously, I tried to move my legs. They were held, but loosely, in something soft. A blanket. Someone had wrapped me in a blanket and carried me here. I attempted to sit up, and my head grazed rock. I stretched out my arms, and my hands touched rock on both sides. That was how I knew where I was.

I was sealed in a chamber of the *broch*.

Shock must act like an anesthetic. I was aware, but as if from a distance, as if I were observing this happening to someone else. Memory returned, but in flashing, disconnected images. Eugene falling forward, his head sinking over his bloodstained collar. Irene struggling with Jim for the gun. Irene a heap of chiffon on the floor. Jim's eyes. The butt of his gun in his uplifted hand as he came toward me. I was aware of horror, but dimly.

Gradually my eyes became used to the darkness. I could even make out a gray rim of light around one side of the slab that sealed my chamber. When I put my hand to the light, I could feel air stirring. I forced myself to move, managing to crowd my legs into a crouching position. With all my strength, I thrust my shoulders against the slab. It held, fixed. Again and again I used my shoulders as a battering ram and struck against the slab, but it was useless. It hardly trembled under my impact.

My head was throbbing. Jim must have struck me several times, because my hair was matted in clotted blood. My shoulders were now too bruised to continue; I had to rest. But even as I lay back, my fingers probed between the stones, searching for a crevice. The walls of the *broch* were a foot and a half thick, and over them centuries had packed the earth hard.

I remembered our coming here, Jim and Irene and I, and how Jim had attempted to move the slab by rocking it back and forth, and how little he had succeeded in dislodging it. Had Jim remembered that day, too, when he was looking for a place to bury me alive?

My mind was still lucid enough to place the incidents together. The one fact that made everything clear was that they were lovers. Or had been. I wondered if Irene was capable of love now, or if Jim could still feel passion for anyone as confused and ill as Irene. But Irene married to Eugene was extraordinarily wealthy. As Eugene's widow, all that wealth would be hers. *And his, if he married her.*

234

Jim must have planned it all. Irene wasn't capable of thinking it through. Irene clung to anyone who offered her love. She must have honestly believed Eugene meant to destroy her, confused as she was by drugs, and guilt-ridden by her succession of infidelities. Jim must have realized how he could play on those fears. The exact opportunity he couldn't have foreseen, but he had waited his chance. He must have known there was only the summer, because after that would come the divorce, and then Irene would have only her settlement, which might not have been worth murdering for, not for Irene as she was.

I was only speculating, but everything fitted. Only the details were unknown. And then there were questions that came to me. Why had he brought me here alive? Why hadn't he killed me at once? Suppose someone were to find me, still alive?

The thought roused me, galvanized me. I put my mouth close to the faint crack of light around the slab and shouted. And shouted. And only when I had used up my supply of energy did I fall back. In my exhaustion reality impinged intermittently, like the brief flare of a match. Eugene is dead. Irene is dead. I will be dead soon, too. Why aren't the police looking for me? How can Jim explain my disappearance? Suppose they are looking for me? Again, I made myself crouch on my knees and put my mouth to the crack and shouted. My voice was hoarse. Who could hear it?

"You're conscious. Good."

Involuntarily I shrank back, as if he could reach me. It was Jim.

235

He said, "There isn't much time for you, Lisette. If you do as you're told, you'll walk out of that hole alive. Otherwise it will be the grave Irene once called it. Remember?"

I remembered.

"Can you hear me?" he said sharply.

"What do you want me to do?" my voice said huskily.

"Good girl," he said. "I want the notes. Tell me where they are."

The notes. So that was why I was alive. He wanted the notes that were hidden in the hem of my skirt. I felt for them. Dampness had seeped through my clothing and made the paper limp, but I could still feel them, stiffening the fabric of my skirt.

"Can you hear me?" he said, again.

"I don't have them," I said. My answer was mechanical.

"Not on you. I know that. I searched you last night. Where did you hide them?"

He was my only chance of survival, through the notes. When he left me, I would be consigned to blackness and death. I had to keep him here, with me, somehow. Stall, talk, give him a reason to stay with me.

I said, "If I tell you, you'll take them and leave me here anyway."

"I wouldn't do that to you, love. I'm fond of you. I didn't want to hurt you."

"You know if you let me go I'll tell the police that you killed Eugene and Irene."

"I didn't kill Irene," he said harshly. "Why should I? I was going to marry her. That was the whole point of the plan. I would marry her once Eugene was dead. But she was too addled to go through with it, and when she saw him die, she turned the gun on herself."

Too addled to go through with it, or unable to bring herself to kill him. Who could know what she felt in her confused mind? I said, "You would have been tried for murder."

"They wouldn't have tried me," he said. "They would never have suspected my part in it if you hadn't barged in. You were supposed to stay in your room. You weren't supposed to see what happened. Because they would never have convicted Irene. A dozen doctors would have testified she was sick. And you and I were there to say how afraid she was of Eugene, how fearful for her life. I had to keep her doped up to believe it, but that was easy, once I was here."

"You gave her the drugs," I said, sickened.

"When she ran out of her own supply. I had to, you see, I couldn't take any chances that she would change her mind, that she would realize what she was doing. I had to keep her scared, or else why would she turn the gun on him?"

"You must have thought your plan would fail, when Eugene went away to the conference."

"It did throw me for a while, but then it worked out even better. I sent him a message and said it was urgent that he come back at once, and signed it with your name. I knew that would bring him home in a hurry. And that would set the stage for Irene to think he had come back secretly to kill her, and she would shoot him to defend her life. It would have worked out just like that, too, if you hadn't come in. If you'd stayed in your room as I told you to, you wouldn't be here now!"

"Then why should you let me out to tell what I saw?"

"What makes you think they would believe you?"

I was stupefied for a moment.

He laughed. "They think you killed both Irene and Eugene, and then in a panic of remorse, threw yourself into the sea."

"But—"

"I had to think fast, that night. I put your prints on the gun, and then tossed it away near the cliffs. I even left one of your shoes there near it, so they'd be sure to come to the correct conclusion."

"What reason?" I said faintly. "What reason could I have?"

"You were in love with Eugene. Anyone could see that. And he certainly seemed to be in love with you. That meeting at the works, when Clarke drove you? But he changed his mind about you, see, and you were desperate. You telephoned him to come back because you had to see him before you left, and when he refused to go away with you, you killed them both."

"No one would think I could murder anyone," I managed to say.

"No? But you made off with strategic material, didn't you? You were bitter enough to sell your country, weren't you? You're still under suspicion, you know."

I couldn't speak.

"Look, I'll help you get away," he said. "Just tell me where the notes are, first. You owe me something, really, after scotching my hope to become a millionaire the easy way."

I had run out of talk. If I refused him now, he would go away, and who would find me? The police must have searched already, and who would walk near the *broch* now? I thought desperately. I must create a few more hours of life.

I said, "You will let me out if I tell you?"

"I promised, didn't I? I told you I liked you very much, Lisette. I really don't want to see you die such an ugly death."

He would have to be mad to think I would believe him, but maybe he knew I didn't and was playing a little game with me, knowing I had no other recourse.

"I hid them between the pages of the book on Eugene's desk. In his room."

"Smart girl." His voice rose, jubilant.

"Aren't you going to let me out?"

"I have to check first, don't I, to make sure you're not lying? Suppose I let you out and the notes weren't there? You don't think I'd let you get away with a stunt like that. The notes better be there, Lisette."

He went away. The silence settled around me. What would he do when he found there were no notes in the book? Come back and force me to tell him where they were? Or just let me die here? No, the notes were too important to him. As he said, they were his only chance of becoming rich quickly, now that Irene was dead.

I thought wildly of ways to escape if he ever returned. When he dug away the slab and bent over me, I would toss dirt in his eyes and blind him momentarily, and then

239

run. Run! How could I run fast enough? My legs were stiff with cramp and cold; how could I run when I could hardly flex them?

A loose stone. If I had a loose stone, I could strike him with it. But I had no strength in my arms anymore; my muscles were as cramped with cold and as useless as my legs.

The cold crept deeper into me. The blanket was useless. How would I die? Would I suffer? Would I lapse into unconsciousness first, before I died? I thought of the story of Silas Marner that I'd read ages ago in high school. Someone in the book, Effie? Effie's mother? had frozen to death in the snow. I remembered reading that she'd felt a lovely, comforting warmth at the end, as the snow covered her. But there was no snow to cover me, only this damp, deadly cold. And anyway, how did George Eliot, who wrote the story, know how it felt to freeze to death in the snow? She had never frozen to death in the snow herself. I began to laugh, and then stopped, afraid. I might be going mad. Would I go mad before I died, would I die raving, and not even know that I was dying?

I thought of Eugene. Eugene was dead. Eugene would never know what happened to me. Eugene loved me. He couldn't have borne it to know what Jim had done to me. I was glad he had died without knowing. I wept. I fell asleep.

Asleep or awake, I heard voices, raised voices, a thump, a heavy fall. Was I reliving the scene in Irene's room, and was it Eugene's body I heard again, falling, Irene's body, falling? I was falling—

Someone was breathing heavily outside the slab. Jim. Jim had come back.

His breath was labored as he worked over the slab, rocking it back and forth, muttering to himself. He was furiously angry, he worked like a man in a furious haste. The tiny line of light to one side of the slab had widened. The slab rocked, and now a thin thread of gray light showed on the other side. My fingers dug into the damp earth. Be ready. A fistful of earth flung into his eyes would stop him, if only for a moment. And after that? How could I run?

The slab was rocking, and the space on either side appeared to grow wider and wider as it moved. It was wide enough now for a man's hand to grasp. I saw the earth-stained fingers gripping the slab. The slab fell over, with a pounding thud.

Light poured in, dazzling my eyes, blinding me. A shape blotted out the light, black against it. I grasped the handful of earth and threw it, but it fell back, showering me.

Muddy fingers reached in for me and gripped me. I screamed.

"Alive," said a grim voice. "You're a lucky girl."

The sweat from his body filled my nostrils along with the cold, incredible freshness of a salt wind. Something familiar—cigars? I was being lifted. A head bent over me, a shining bald head.

The birdwatcher.

🌿 *17*

When I opened my eyes, I was in bed. In a hospital bed: no other kind has the sheets drawn so crisply and tightly that you cannot move your arms. I moved my head cautiously. Protective bars were raised on either side, and beyond, a nurse was shaking down a thermometer.

The gray slate roofs of Lerwick slanted below my window. Sunlight, the painted walls, all dazzled my eyes after the relentless blackness of the *broch*.

He was sitting quietly in a corner, dozing, I think. The birdwatcher, a hard, stocky monolith of a man with about as much expression on his hacked-out granite features, his bare scalp a pale, polished moon.

He heard my exclamation, and he was on his feet. "Don't get scared. I'm friend, not foe."

I tried to clear my throat. I said hoarsely, "I didn't kill them. Jim put the gun in my hand, afterward."

"There now," said the nurse, and put the thermometer under my tongue.

"We have an idea what happened," said the bird-watcher. "Mr. Farrar told us."

"Mr. Farrar?" The thermometer fell from my mouth. "He's alive?" I choked with sudden tears, and the nurse replaced the thermometer patiently, saying, "There now," again, and, "You must expect to be weak for a while yet."

"But he *is* alive?" I mumbled imploringly. "You spoke to him?"

"The first bullet just grazed him," said the bird-watcher. "Mrs. Farrar wasn't much of a shot. The second missed the jugular by a fraction. What he couldn't say he wrote down. We kept his condition a secret so we could keep an eye on Baird. And he led us to you."

"Does Eugene know—" I mumbled some more, until the nurse stopped me.

"He knows all about you," she said. "Please to be still. I have other patients to do."

I subsided. And then I remembered the notes.

"The notes—"

The birdwatcher was on his feet. He took the thermometer from my mouth and pushed it brusquely at the nurse and waved her out of the room. "What about the notes?"

I was silent, suddenly wary. He said he was friend, not foe, and he had saved my life, but who was he?

I made him tell me, before I said another word. He showed me badge and papers. He worked for Larris Foundry, taking up where the FBI had left off. They had hired him to watch me, to see if I made a move to sell the notes, or if someone tried to buy them from me. He had almost given up and decided I didn't have them, only Eugene had asked him to stay on for the time he was away.

He was not a storybook detective, always adroit, impossibly elusive. He had shown his hand on board ship when he had lifted my pocketbook and then replaced it, when he had tripped me to recover that scrap of paper that had nothing on it but the addresses of some of my fellow passengers. He had stolen into the house the night of the Coast Guard Ball and made enough noise so that Irene heard him. And he had followed me to the Royal Hotel and then had to knock out the woman who'd posed as Judy, in order to search her and her room. But he had followed Jim to the *broch* when Jim had returned, after not finding the notes, and pulled a gun on him and handcuffed him to the van while he dug away the slab and saved me. Maybe he was less than storybook adroit, but he was tenacious and persistent, and as he talked, his ugly bald head grew increasingly beautiful to me.

I still insisted that he telephone Eugene in his Edinburgh hospital so I could talk to him before I disclosed where the notes were. Both Eugene and I found speech difficult at first, he because his throat was still bandaged, I because I could not believe he was really alive. He said the birdwatcher was what he said he was. Someone in the government had been in touch with him before I came, someone high up in security, and asked for Eugene's help in watching me, and Eugene had agreed. He was to help the birdwatcher, whose name was Coppola, maintain his cover, and under no circumstances was Eugene to let me know I was being watched. Mr. Coppola had studied ornithology at City College, and had himself suggested that he pretend to be a birdwatcher. Besides, it really was his hobby.

Eugene said, "It wasn't difficult to maintain the fiction at first, when I didn't know you. Later, it was a rotten business, and I wanted to chuck it, but I'd given my word."

I understood. Eugene was that kind of man.

"Then I should give the notes to Mr. Coppola."

"Get the blasted things back to Beale," he said.

Eugene's nurse took the phone from him and told me he had talked enough, so I replaced my own phone and told the birdwatcher where the notes were. He took my skirt from its hanger and dug down, and I saw his incredulous face as he drew out that mangled, faded blue strip that had caused such anguish in so many quarters. He at once rushed out, to wire or phone, and was back in a short while, looking happy, to say good-bye.

"It's such an oddball story," he said, "they're bound to believe it. They'll be in touch, when you're better."

We shook hands, and I thanked him with fervor, and he blushed and said, "Always like to see a job turn out right."

I had a concussion and a chest congestion, but they cleared up nicely, and I was able to leave the hospital in a few days. My mother called and wanted to fly to Scotland to take me home, but I told her I was fine and able to come home by myself. Uncle Willy did not call. My mother said he was taking Irene's death very hard. Eugene had used his influence to tone down the newspaper accounts, but murder is always lurid.

I went to Edinburgh on my way home. Eugene was able to move about freely by then, although he still had to ration his speech. He was able to put his arms around me and hold me as if he had done it all his life, and it was most natural.

"I wish I could have spared you the mess," he said. "You can expect the newspapers to be after you for a while, but they'll drop you at the first hint of some new sensation."

The same security agency that had asked for Eugene's help in covering for the birdwatcher had seen to it that nothing was leaked about the notes. Now that they were back in Beale's hands, a release would go out to the newspapers soon that a small piece of information vital to the ABM program and presumed mislaid had turned up after all. This was for my sake, to protect me. Edna had written about Beale's reaction to their recovery: relief, intermingled with an explosion about my criminal stupidity. But I no longer cared.

"Where are you going now, Lisette? What are your plans?"

"I'm going home. I'll find a job. And try to soften what happened for my mother and Uncle Willy."

"I'll be in New York as soon as I can travel, and I'll do what I can." There was a pause. "Will I see you?"

My throat tightened, and I couldn't speak. I nodded.

He said, "It isn't as if either of us were responsible for that night. We were their victims. It would be wrong to waste any more of our lives in feelings of guilt. I don't want to do that, Lisette. Do you?"

I shook my head.

He said as he had once before, "You won't let Irene come between us?"

I had thought about it long and hard those days in the hospital. Maybe, with time, it would be possible for us to forget her, enough at least so that we could be happy. Nothing we did could hurt her anymore. "No, Gene, I think it's going to be all right."

We kissed good-bye. Once before we had kissed good-bye, and I thought it final, and the kiss was enveloped in fear and suspicion and unhappiness. This time it evoked that mist-covered island again, and its black peat furrows and constant winds, its bogs and low clouds and pale sunshine, but now it seemed beautiful to me, and full of promise.